The Long Drive
and other mysteries

CHARLES MICHELL

Cover and illustrations by Mary Woodin

Privately published
© Charles Michell 2020
Produced for the author
by Matthew Mullett (Publisher)
Illustrations © Mary Woodin

Printed and bound by Biddles Books Limited
Castle House, East Winch Road, Blackborough End
King's Lynn, Norfolk
PE32 1SF

ISBN: 978–1–913663–72–8

To Frida and Matilda

Foreword

Motoring along a narrow Suffolk lane I regularly pass the entrance to a long drive, its gate held up by nettles and tangled bushes. The drive is neglected and still. It rounds a bend and disappears through the trees. I imagine it leads to a dark, stone-built house, probably Victorian, dilapidated, occupied by a lonely soul unable to halt its decline. I wonder who this person may be, how far the drive stretches and what is at the end of it. I feel a sense of unease whenever I pass the gate.

A ghost story suggests itself and it became my intention to write one. After all it would give me something to do during the first phase of the Covid pandemic lockdown in that glorious summer of 2020. The warmth of those days was certainly not compatible with disturbing thoughts and it was not surprising that the story took a different turn from the one I had expected. But in spite of the sunshine and birdsong I still could not avoid the eeriness of the story leading me on to its mysterious ending.

All these stories are drawn from imagination and, sometimes, from real-life experiences of my own. I hope the excitement they have aroused in me will be shared by readers of these tales.

Contents

The Long Drive

Hammonds were well-known in the West Midlands as a small publishing business run by Henry Hammond, the grandson of the Founder. Its level of business had remained static for the past few years but its staff had generally stuck with it, glad of the security that loyalty and long service bring and the prospect of a comfortable pension upon retirement.

Bob Hatherly and Colin Gray worked together as colleagues in Hammonds' Accounts Department. The job was unexciting but regular and predictable enough to guarantee a break at lunchtime to allow the two men to visit the local pub for some light relief and restoration. Their daily shifts would end at 5 pm, each returning home by bus to the opposite ends of town for an evening of tea and television with their wives. This was the routine that both men practised contentedly as the decades passed—until retirement loomed.

Each man lived in an unremarkable but respectable district, handy for shops and buses, close to a community centre, church and public gardens.

Colin's house was a two-bedroomed dwelling in a long Edwardian terrace, which faced similar houses with small front gardens and a privet hedge. Visitors would find his house by following the numbers on the doors—even numbers on this side, odd numbers on the other—as they walked past the identical frontages, each door with porch and a number beneath a central bell. The bell at the Grays' house had not worked for some time but that was of little consequence since the Grays had few visitors and found fulfilment in each other's company. Their house had brown-painted window-frames and was without any obvious welcoming feature, save for the light bulb which hung on a cable in the porch: no shade, just a naked bulb of low wattage, dimly set back in the porch. Hilda made sure it was turned on every night when Colin returned from work—not that Colin needed it to find his own house, but just so that some light would be there to welcome him home. Hilda never failed: the light was on whenever Colin returned. As he clicked his key in the lock and pushed open the door Hilda would invariably call out "Is that you, dear?" It could only have been Colin, nobody else had a key, but it was reassuring for Hilda to know that he was safely home. The porch light could then be turned off.

Colin's ten-year-old car was parked in the street occupying a space right outside the house in a bay which it seldom vacated. Hilda had begun to comment on the age of the car and how they should think about getting a new one but Colin had always kept it well serviced and maintained and it had never let them down. Besides he had never been interested in cars and, so long as the car got them to where they wanted to go, what was the point of a new one? This was typical of Colin. He had few interests outside work and fewer ambitions. He would have liked to upgrade his car in theory, just to please Hilda, but his modest salary covered their lifestyle without frills and anything which upset the running of his organised budget, such as saving up, would be inconvenient at best. Colin never took his car to work, public transport being less stressful, so the car remained, little used, sitting outside the front door.

Hilda was inwardly more ambitious than Colin, but she did not like to show it. She knew Colin's job was paramount and that he was meticulous about living within his means. So she asked for very little. She noticed that their house had become quite shabby, nothing having been spent on its redecoration for many years. The passageway through to the living room where they sat each evening was dimly lit and the floor of melancholy Edwardian tiles did nothing to lift it. Deep down Hilda would have loved to spruce up the house and to have a car more in keeping with modern trends but she accepted that such things would remain a dream until Colin's retirement on a decent pension. Then maybe the dream would become real and there would be money to spend on a few additional comforts. For the time being, everything would have to wait.

Hilda's day followed a weekly routine: shopping, a trip to the library for a racy novel, a bus ride to visit her friend Elsie Hobbs for a chat or a trip to the Council offices maybe to complain about the bus timetable. She invented a purpose for every day, anything that would soak up the hours till Colin returned home and they could settle down for their evening meal.

Hilda and Colin had no children, but they had each other, spending their annual summer holiday at the same boarding house on the West Coast they had known for much of their forty years of marriage. It was one of the few occasions in the year when they used their car for any length of time. Colin did the driving while Hilda was unerring in her map-reading. For their two week break they drove to deserted beaches, walked the cliff paths, attended the local cinema and took in a variety show on the pier. Without any desire to go abroad, they enjoyed the pleasures of a traditional English seaside resort, safe with the diet they understood and the bracing sea breezes they loved. In many ways it was a lifestyle to envy, familiar surroundings being the source of their enjoyment, their love for one another the security they needed.

Bob and Molly Hatherly led more adventurous lives. Molly was Treasurer of her local branch of the Women's Institute: Bob had joined a team of bell-ringers which practised on Thursday evenings and rang the bells of Saint Ethelreda's on the following Sunday. Like the Grays the couple seldom travelled abroad but enjoyed the occasional bus tour around Scotland or a trip to the South Coast linking up with friends for outings. Sometimes they would go out for meals. They kept up with the latest film releases and attended concerts streamed from the Albert Hall at their local cinema.

The two couples had met socially often enough for the wives to develop a firm bond. The question of retirement for both men was on the horizon and the change that this would make to their daily lives was being discussed. The Grays, as inseparable from their home as they were from each other, would remain where they were. The Hatherlys were talking about moving away from the area, further out into the country, for fresh air and space. The idea of involvement in a village community appealed to them. It would also bring Bob greater opportunities to ring bells in churches away from busy urban centres thereby avoiding the complaints of intolerant residents. Retirement would not come easy for either couple but they resolved to stay in touch, and the Hatherlys promised not to move too far away.

It was Hilda who took the prospect of change worst of all and this may have partly led to a breakdown in her health. For some months she was ill at ease before a wasting disease was diagnosed. Colin supported her as well as he could but her health declined until she became bedridden. It seemed the only thing that kept her alive was the thought of leaving Colin on his own. She knew how much Colin needed her… how much they needed each other.

Bob and Molly visited her with flowers and optimistic thoughts endeavouring to cheer her up while lightening the burden for Colin who dreaded the loneliness that her passing would bring. Hilda

Gray died peacefully at home with Colin holding her hand, their wedding photograph on the table beside the bed next to a jug of chrysanthemums which Bob and Molly Hatherly had brought. Her funeral was a modest affair in a churchyard ten miles away, at the village where she grew up. Elsie Hobbs had arranged the flowers: a few members of Hilda's remote family attended, and a few from Colin's workplace. Bob gave a short address. The coffin was gently lowered into the earth and Hilda was gone. To Colin she was irreplaceable.

For some months Colin's work was his only consolation, though Bob's imminent retirement would soon destroy that as well. Colin would return each evening to a lonely house and click his key in the door, the naked bulb now hanging unlit in the porch and with no human voice to welcome him home. He had never been one for socialising so Colin would just spend his evenings at home, cook a simple snack and wait until the television news had ended. The routine which Hilda had imposed would then allow him to retire to bed. Hilda had been the only woman in his life and Bob one of his very few male friends as they worked together down the years in Hammonds' Accounts Department.

While Bob remained a workmate Colin's life still had some meaning but when Bob's final day at work arrived Colin felt a new sense of bereavement. The day following Bob's retirement Colin turned up at the office and sat at his desk on his own. Hammonds had generously kept his place open during his months of absence caring for Hilda but, without Bob, the job had effectively finished for Colin. A replacement was being appointed to fill Bob's place but to endure a new partner at work left Colin in a state of bottomless depression. He arranged for his own retirement from Hammonds, mindful that it would leave his own life without purpose. But without Bob work satisfaction had ceased.

He now faced a bleak future, finding past memories more important than his present existence. Weekdays passed slowly but at weekends he would take the car from its slot outside his house for a pilgrimage to Hilda's grave, where he would sit silently reliving their holidays and times together. When he felt it was time to return home he would say a little prayer over her grave. "See you again soon, dear" he would murmur before sinking into his car for the lonely drive back.

The street where Colin and Hilda had lived for all of their married life was not near a shopping centre or a sports ground and those who parked in the street tended to be those who lived there. There were no dedicated parking bays but there was an understanding that residents would park outside their own house and a space would be left clear for each one. So it came as a surprise and a considerable annoyance that, on returning home one weekend, Colin found a car which he did not recognise parked in the space he usually occupied. He was forced to park at the end of the street and walk back. The car occupying his normal bay looked new, a dark blue mini-saloon, a Leopard 500 (so it read on the driver's door), quite distinctive in this street of modest vehicles. But what puzzled Colin was that he did not know of anyone who had bought a new car and, if they had, they would have known not to park it in his space. But it didn't really matter. It would be gone by the morning.

On Monday morning, the car was still there and hadn't moved by the time Colin checked on it that evening. Annoyed that someone had blatantly abused the street rules he peered in through the driver's window. The seats were clear. There was a roadmap in the pocket of the front passenger door but nothing else he could see and no clue as to who the owner could be. The car stayed where it was and as days went by Colin could only speculate. Maybe it belonged to someone who has gone overseas for a while, who was not conversant with the ways of this street. Who could tell?

Colin weighed up its presence with mixed emotions. It was first a gross impertinence that someone should have parked in his bay without notice or permission but on the other hand he felt satisfied by the sight of a sleek new car outside his house and not someone else's old wreck. Every morning he looked out but the car was still there. As days passed, he accepted the situation. It would go eventually. He tried to put it out of his mind but its presence kept reminding him of something, perhaps of his own shortcomings. He could surely afford to trade his car in, get a smarter one. He could have done so long ago when Hilda was alive, if only he had been a bit more flexible. Ah, yes, "if only", he thought, she would have loved that… but it was too late now.

One day, out of the blue, the postman brought Colin a handwritten letter addressed in ink and it boosted him more than anything had done for weeks. It came from 'The Glebe, Flaxford Road, Easton Darnley'. It was from Molly Hatherly and to his delight it invited him to visit them in their new home tucked away in the country about seventy miles to the east. They had been doing work on the interior ('not much to the garden yet') and the rear rooms and bedrooms were now comfortable enough for guests. How would he like to stay with them for three nights? The rest of the house was still "a bit rough", Molly confessed, but he ought not to be put off by that.

Colin telephoned Molly at once to accept. It was just the break he needed. Molly explained that an old friend of Bob's, over from the States, would also be staying as a guest for a few days. "We'll be an awesome foursome" Molly laughed. "It's not hard to find us: go through Flaxford heading in the direction of Easton Darnley and after slightly less than a mile you will see our white gateposts on the left. I'll put some directions in the post."

This was a morale-booster for Colin, to be catching up with old friends. Three days in the country would be an adventure. He cherished the opportunity to get out of his area and into the open country, away from the dull routine of the town, to savour a new experience though he was really a townsman at heart and knew the predictability of the town was not always present in the rural areas. He knew that well, but that only enhanced his thrill of expectation. So long as he prepared the way and took his time, a two-hour drive eastwards should hold no terrors. He had a good map and had received the further directions from Molly that she had promised. "Bob's friend will be arriving early evening, so why don't you get here around 5 pm? The light should last till then, so you won't have to drive in the dark."

Colin spent time preparing the route. It was only three miles between Flaxford and Easton Darnley, and he was sure he would have no difficulty finding the white gates to the Hatherly house along that road. He felt his pioneering spirit swelling as the day of his departure approached.

But there was yet to be one curious event to take place before Colin left. It was on the day immediately preceding his trip into the country. As he drew up the blinds to look out of his front window, a different scene confronted him. He stepped back to take another look. The parking bay right outside his house was empty. The car had gone... the sleek Leopard 500, which had occupied his space all these weeks, had vanished overnight, noiselessly and without warning. From his window Colin surveyed the street to see if it was parked in another bay to offend someone else, but no, it was plainly gone. "What a relief," he thought as he drove his car back from the end of the street to reclaim his own parking bay at last, "but ironic that it should have been removed just as I am about to go away. Typical, of course: that's what fate does to you. It will be even more ironic if someone else comes along and fills the space in those days when I'm gone." He was on the other hand genuinely pleased to have his bay back. When he returned from his visit to the Hatherlys, with luck he will be able to park in his own space again. From that point of view it was an opportune moment for this to happen.

Blue sky and dry motoring conditions greeted Colin's departure. He had left in good time only stopping at the local mini-market to pick up some house presents for the Hatherlys. Although this used up the surplus time he had reserved for hold-ups he was still ahead of schedule. Now on the high road heading east he felt happy and confident. He had his road map to back him up but he had learnt the way and everything went according to plan as Colin left the suburban roads behind and headed off into the country. The traffic thinned, open fields lay motionless in the pale afternoon sunshine and lines of oaks along the roadside kept him company. Colin had time to think. He thought of his holidays with Hilda, driving to the coast and their walks together along the cliffs. It felt strange to be driving on his own, without Hilda there in the front seat to guide him, unerring in her skills at map-reading and her sense of direction. He was no good at that kind of thing. That was why he had had to spend so much time learning the route this time. His thoughts of her and the good times they'd spent together made the miles pass quicker. He hardly noticed that the light was growing dimmer and he must be nearing his destination. Then he saw it. Just where he would have expected it to be, lucky he'd been paying enough attention, a signpost marking the turning to FLAXFORD. Colin turned off the major road. Eight miles then to Flaxford and then a mile or two further on and he was there. Probably not much more than twenty minutes. It hardly mattered that a little light rain had started to fall. He would be spot on time.

Colin had his sidelights on. They would be adequate for Flaxford where streetlights would guide him through. He followed the road, his morale high. Then suddenly he spotted something ahead which sent his spirits tumbling. Colin pulled up at the metal notice which barred his way. It read: ROAD AHEAD

CLOSED FOR REPAIRS. DIVERSION. Colin's mind emptied as he tried to think what he ought to do next. His only option, as far as he could see, was to follow the Diversion. But where were they diverting him to? How did they know where he wanted to go? How would he recognise where he was when they had brought him back on his road again, if indeed they ever would? But, worse still, was it one of those Diversions that had no ending? Colin considered breaking through the barrier, but was reluctant to run the risk of turning up at the Hatherlys in a police van. So, anxiously, he swung the wheel to the right and plunged off down a country lane. And into the unknown.

It was as confusing as he had expected. At each fork or junction in the road he lingered in case he departed from the diversion route. He feared to speed up in case he missed the way, though he was conscious of the passing time and he was constantly reminding himself of how late it was getting. He felt an urge to stop and consult the map but just as he was about to do so he became aware of a car coming up fast behind him. The driver flashed its lights. Without a stretch for overtaking on windy roads like these, Colin moved on briskly and took himself off the road into the next minor turning, signed "Church Farm only", to allow the car behind to pass. On occasions like this one thing is certain: that the impatient car behind will be turning into that same road. There was no escape. The headlights behind him followed hard on his tail. Colin proceeded a short distance up the lane and stopped. A 4x4 crept up alongside him and halted. "Can I help at all?" called out a voice with an overload of sarcasm. "I'm trying to find Easton Darnley," Colin replied. "You won't find it up here", shouted the unmistakeable farmer. "Why don't you read the effing signpost." And with a mud-flinging spin of the wheel his vehicle took off up the lane towards Church Farm.

Controlling his frustration, Colin resumed his route. He entered the village of Hedstone and pulled in at the pub. At least there was light by which to read his map, space to take his bearings and maybe some local information to be had which would set him on his way. It was plainly not a busy evening at the Crown. A gormless-looking boy behind the bar, the kind who stands there on sufferance to earn a few pounds while waiting to go up to Uni, seemed incapable of understanding Colin's problem. "I'll get my father," he said. For several minutes nothing happened, then the boy returned. "He's a bit caught up at the moment" he said, "but he doesn't know

Easton Darnley anyway and he doesn't think he can help". That was a brilliant waste of time, thought Colin. He already had the map out on the table and was studying it when a local voice broke in. "Where're you trying to get to?" said the regular sitting alone at a far table. Colin told him. "You want to go back to the Flaxford Road" he advised. "Yes, but it's closed," said Colin, "that's why I'm here... in Hedstone... which I am trying to find on the map. What I need to know is how I get from here to Easton Darnley." The slow old local had plainly never ventured far from Hedstone (and, by the look of him, probably not far from the bar at the Crown either) and the help he was so keen to give added very little to solving Colin's problem. Studying the map took longer than Colin would have wished but together they devised a route. All being well Colin was on his last lap.

With rain falling heavier now, windscreen wipers and demisters in full use and no moon to lift the darkness of the night, driving conditions were far from ideal. But Colin now had a fair grasp of his intended route and, so long as he did not miss a turning, he could follow his notes which were sitting there on the front passenger seat. So long as he did not miss a turning. Admittedly, distances are hard to judge from a map and miles appear longer if one is not familiar with the road. Colin made steady progress but was all the time conscious that he was now terribly late and the poor Hatherlys must be wondering what had happened to him… or whether he was coming at all. Had they given him the right directions? Had they described the house adequately? Had they overestimated Colin's competence to find his way in the dark? It was frustrating in the extreme, and the pressure was getting to him, but he could do no more than battle on hoping for something to turn up. So long as he followed his route there was no need to despair. It seemed much further than he had expected and the thought nagged him that he may indeed have missed a turning… especially one a few minutes ago, where the road layout was confusing and he had had to take a calculated guess. If he had got it wrong at that junction, the rest of his plan would be useless and he would be utterly lost. Panic was not far away when, without warning, his headlights picked up a signpost… EASTON DARNLEY 2.

Relief at last! Colin could not decide for certain which road he was on, or which side of Easton Darnley he was, but if he was on the Flaxford side only two miles from Easton Darnley he must be very close to the Hatherlys' house. Very close.

Then through the rain and the blackness of the night, across the road, he saw an entrance. "Look out for white gates" Molly had told him. These were not the kind of white gates he had expected. Two gateposts, which seemed white enough in the dark, framed a driveway through a mass of trees and Colin instinctively nosed his car into the gap. On one side a metal gate leaned backwards, sunk by one hinge into a muddy bank and stuck in thick undergrowth. Colin hesitated at the entrance but a driveway stretched ahead inviting him to whatever lay at the end of it. He was launched now and, even if he had been inclined to do so, he was not turning back. If this was the Hatherlys' house then he had arrived. He drove slowly along the narrow track, seeing and hearing nothing except for the branches of bare trees clicking in the wind above him and drops of rain falling heavily on the roof of his car. Grass grew along the centre of the drive and incidental shrubs brushed the sides of his vehicle. It seemed a long way without a light appearing and Colin wondered if anyone was living in the house at the end of the drive, assuming there was a house there at all. At last the trees thinned and the drive widened and Colin, emerging into the open, saw the outline of a house, facing sideways to his direction. It was impossible to judge its condition in the dark, but Colin could detect a brick exterior—a period building, maybe Edwardian—formal without being grand and a bit more austere than what he would have associated with the Hatherlys. There some light from a window at the back of the house, mostly obscured by blinds or curtains, but no light from the body of the house. The only other light came from a single bulb hanging from a cable in the porch.

Colin drew up on the far side of the gravel which ringed a grass circle and provided parking in front of the house. He walked tentatively over the wet grass to the dimly-lit lobby. Was this really the Hatherlys' house, he kept asking himself? They had always been a bit more adventurous than he had been in spite of Hilda's promptings to smarten up the house a bit. If only he had listened to her it would have brightened their lives and made Hilda happier... but it was too late now. Colin found a bell and pushed it. He could not hear it ring, and nobody came. Maybe it was not working. He looked through the letterbox. A thin light at the end of the passageway which stretched ahead was the only clue to anyone's presence in the house. He did not fail to notice, though, that some paint pots and decorating materials had been placed just inside the door but it was impossible to see how recent they were. It would certainly cheer the place up, he thought, but who was he to advise, since he had done precious little about it himself when Hilda was alive? But he must not dwell in the past: it made him feel uneasy; unease increased by the strong suspicion that he must be at the wrong house. This could surely not be the Hatherlys' home. How he wished he had asked Molly for a fuller description of their house. The Glebe, it was called. What the hell was a glebe anyway? Why had he not looked it up before he left home to give him a decent clue? All that preparation, and he had omitted the most important details. Anyway this was not a glebe, surely not. He was at the wrong house. Whoever lived here, if anyone did, it was plainly not the Hatherlys. He must leave, quickly before anyone accused him of snooping around their house after dark. Quickly, before the house reminded him of any more of his past failings—of how he had let Hilda down. He must leave at once.

His footsteps quickened across the grass circle, he jumped into his car and slammed the door shut. Feeling more secure, he completed the circuit in front of the house, before selecting a muddy roadway for his retreat. There was no time to look around. He wanted to accelerate, to escape as fast as possible, to get away from the house. He was afraid of slipping off the track. That would be catastrophic. Colin held his nerve, travelling slowly enough to keep control but fast enough to effect his escape. Happily the track seemed a bit wider and the trees not so oppressive this time. He must have nearly reached the main road. And there it was. He could just make out the whiteness of the gate, increasingly obvious as he approached. Strangely, larger than he remembered, no longer leaning into the undergrowth but upright now. The tall metal gate was standing across the drive, barring his exit, preventing passage in or out. Colin froze in his driving seat barely able to stop the car. For interminable seconds he gazed at the barrier ahead as cold terror slowly overwhelmed him. There was no doubt about it, he could see it clearly: the gate was padlocked, solid and firmly shut. There was no way forward, and no way out.

—

"I am so glad you made it all right, Stan", said Molly to their newly arrived American guest. "We are a bit out in the sticks here but we are really happy you've found us. Did you have a terrible journey?" "Yup," said Stan, "pretty bad, but I'm getting used to your country roads and driving on the 'wrong' side."

"Not to mention the foul weather", added Bob Hatherly, pouring his old friend a stiff Bourbon and ginger. "You did well to find us on a night like this."

"To be honest," said Stan, "I'm relieved to be here. I gave up driving in the UK years ago, except for trips like this to see you all. It was too hairy and I spent so much time looking at the road and trying to figure out your roundabouts, I never had time to see the country properly. And driving in your cities was suicidal." Stan drew his hand across his throat. "No way," he said. "So I leave the car in an unrestricted street somewhere and use your buses and trains. You can see much more of the country that way and I have really enjoyed the few weeks I have been over here this time. By the way, did you say there was another guest staying with you tonight?" Bob and Molly looked at each other. "He is so late, he must either be lost or he has forgotten to come, probably the latter. We'll give him a few more minutes but, frankly, we have already given him up for tonight."

Stan took a more positive view. "It's a wild night out there," he said, "and I nearly missed your entrance drive myself. If you guys have a flashlight or something I'll take it down to the gate and hang it there. If it's powerful enough it will show your guest the way in. I can do that for you, no problem." Then, seeing Bob and Molly resisting his generous offer, he added, "No, really, I'd be happy to do that."

—

Colin gazed in horror at the gate. The only way out of this nightmare was back, back up the track in the dark with only reversing lights to guide him, the rear window misted up, his wing mirrors obscured by rain. Colin threw the car into reverse and lurched backwards. His numbed feet could hardly feel the pedals and his body shook at what hidden dangers lay behind him along the driveway. Each rev, it seemed, had to be corrected by a forward motion to keep his line straight. He was consumed by the possibility that someone may have followed him down the track and that a face might suddenly appear at the window, or that there was someone approaching him from the gate. He could not accelerate for fear of a wheel-spin. Occasionally he became certain that eyes were watching him through the windscreen. He would swing round in his seat… but there was no one there. He saw a figure in the drive—but it was only his car lights playing with a shadow in the pine trees. He was certain he heard voices but they were just the chatter of silver birch twigs above his head. Colin passed an eternity in fear that somebody would block his way, somebody interested to know what he was doing on their property in the dark. How could he explain himself? Or what if there was nobody there at all and he was actually alone?

At last he felt his rear wheels strike firmer ground and saw miraculously that he was nearly back at the house. Relief that he had reached the top of the drive made him relax slightly. He reversed the last few paces towards the circle in front of the house, pushed the gear lever forward and stopped the car. Collapsing in his seat he took a deep breath, turned his headlights off and looked vacantly around him. For countless seconds he noticed nothing and felt nothing, hardly remembering where he was but, as reality returned, he became aware that something in the general scene had changed. The light in the porch was out.

Colin was in no state to judge why. He cast his eyes more carefully in that direction… and then at something that was standing outside the house. A glint thrown up by his sidelights nailed Colin's attention now. It was the glint of a car, a reflection from the bonnet of a smart saloon car parked outside the front door. Fascinated, Colin shifted himself from his driver's seat and stood gazing towards it. He could see it was of a dark colour, maybe deep blue, well maintained and polished. But more than that: he recognised its make and its familiar lines; he knew what would be written on the driver's door— 'Leopard 500' it would say.

For a moment Colin stood paralysed beside his car. Any thought he may have had about ringing the doorbell disappeared in an instant. Who was living at the house? Who, who was in there?

He did not have long to wait. A light—a strong and powerful light—had appeared at the front door and was spilling into the porch, then moving outside the lobby and filling the trees around the grass circle. The beam turned till its arc swung slowly in Colin's direction. Within seconds it would find him and then he would be pinned into its halo of light. It was moving inescapably towards him. Colin found himself trapped in its beam, unable to move. The light approached him closer… closer… closer.

He tried to shout, but no sound came. He knew what he wanted to say, though he could merely mouth the words. Staring into the light, he mumbled inaudibly:

"Is that you, dear?" he said.

—

 Bob and Molly Hatherly settled into their armchairs and waited for Stan to return.

The Rain Forest

When the sun falls in the Caribbean it falls fast. From his balcony above the sugar cane and banana trees, away down the hillside where sloping palm trees evidenced the strength of the prevailing winds, Bob Baxter sat back on his wicker chair and gazed at the sunset. Out to sea the air was clear. Silver light drew a path across the ocean to the horizon. Bob kept his eyes fixed on the setting sun waiting for that split second when the sun vanished from view and a green flash signalled the end of another day in paradise. He had seen the flash many times before but conditions had to be right to catch this atmospheric phenomenon. Once he had had the satisfaction of seeing it, having trained himself not to blink at the crucial moment, he could prepare for the traditional happy hour and wait for his guests to appear before Vincent brought in the final meal of the day.

Vincent had been with Bob since Bob first landed on the island thirty-four years before. Bob had fallen in love with the island at first sight and had bought himself a house high up on the mountain side with panoramic views of the lower slopes. The flat ocean spread out as a backdrop, huge, expressionless and asleep. He knew well that down below on the coast, or by the jetty in the small town of St James, the sea could sometimes swell vigorously. But it was calm now and the forecast was for settled weather.

Bob had been studying the lead-blue sea from his balcony a lot that afternoon. At one point just a single fishing vessel was crossing it, as motionless as the hands of a clock, standing in the same position for minutes as he looked but, when he took his eyes off it momentarily and looked again, the boat had moved on a fraction, just as time does when not being watched. The sun, the wonders of the ocean, the silence… all these inspire the imagination. They are what attract the visitor to small island life in the Caribbean. Bob's guests had hit it exactly right.

"Where are our guests?" asked Bob, as Vincent started to lay out the dishes on the table, "they haven't joined me for drinks tonight. Could you remind them that dinner is ready and I'm expecting them for a decent snifter before we sit down".
"I not see them since this morning," Vincent replied. "They go out and I not see them no more".

—

Bob's niece, Alison, and her newly-married husband, Ryan, had arrived on the island two days before. Porters had carried their luggage off the small boat when it docked at the jetty and transferred it to an ancient black Cadillac which the young couple piled into, excited by the novelty of a scene entirely different from the London streets they trod daily on their way to work. They were engaging the small island life for the first time, with its simple greetings, its carefree ways and its haphazard rules of parking. They were instantly beguiled by the unpretentious feel of the island and the sense that nothing much had changed here for a generation. It was that glorious sense of informality and freedom that thrilled them as their ancient taxi rattled its way up the curling road towards the house on the hill where Bob, Alison's uncle, lived.

Alison was already beginning to understand why a man of independent character like Bob would have come here in the first place and why he would have been reluctant to leave. To relax, to shut off from the turbulent world, to free himself from the city life... was it not obvious that almost anyone could fall for these unhurried ways, surrounded by all this beauty, vivid colours and timelessness? Uncle Bob had picked a winner here, she thought, where he could spend his days untroubled by traffic jams, unwanted telephone calls and the frustrations of maintaining a property in an unpredictable English climate. Simplicity was seeping into Alison as she contemplated the two whole weeks that she and Ryan would be spending with Uncle Bob.

"I'm Mayhew," the taxi-driver told them, as they left the jetty. "You from England? How long you here?" "Yes, we left home very early this morning: it's been a long journey but it's wonderful to be here. We'll be exploring a bit, perhaps some other islands, but probably we'll be staying two weeks. Have you always lived on the island, Mr Mayhew?" "Oh, yes, ma'am. You know, my name is Mayhew, that's my first name, I'm Mayhew Bird, that's my full name, but I always known as Mayhew. You call me Mayhew, ma'am."

The taxi reached a plateau on the hill with some effort and turned into an unmade road pointing straight up the mountain with Mayhew keeping the car tyres on the parallel concrete strips which formed the track. Small wooden-tiled houses raised on stones perched alongside the roadway each with its area of ground. A chicken, a pig, a cooking pot and a chair lurked beneath a banana tree outside one of them. A radio blared a message of hope. No cares, no worries, just let the sun come up, get through the day and wait for the sun to sink. 'This', to Alison and Ryan, was 'the life', a life seemingly ignorant of the world outside. No wonder Uncle Bob had settled here. After moments of thrill and anticipation the taxi passed through gates and pulled up at a traditional island house, protected by a wall of bougainvillea, built of local stone to the upper floor and then of wooden slats and exterior shutters above. From his balcony Bob had heard the taxi mounting the hill for some minutes and he stood there waving a welcome to his visitors while Vincent greeted them, pulled the luggage out of the car and showed them up the flight of wooden steps that led on to the balcony.

With scarcely time to recover from the shock and wonder of their new environment the visitors found themselves seated on padded rattan chairs overawed by the beauty of land and ocean spread before them. They had entered a fantasy. Bob poured them a cocktail of rum, fruit juice, a chaser with a vicious kick, ice and more ice till the weariness of their travels disappeared. Already they were feeling they knew this place: it was theirs. The anxieties and inhibitions of home life had vanished and they could relax as never before. Perhaps this was the real world after all.

They talked passionately at dinner to the sound of tree frogs and cicadas heralding the night. Chatter was about the family, how everyone was, what they were doing, who had grown the tallest, achieved most success. From Bob the guests wanted to know what island life was like, how he occupied his days, did he long to see the bright lights again and what, if anything, was missing in this blissful existence? Were there any drawbacks to this untroubled life? Did he ever have an urge to leave the island, for short periods, or forever?

—

To Alison and Ryan this lifestyle was idyllic: it was impossible to understand why the whole world would not want to live like this. But then, if they did, they would kill the very thing that made it magical. That peace, that gentleness, that security—and the sun would come up and the sun would go down, and you could sit on the balcony and watch it.

Sleep comes easily in this climate. Nights are interrupted only by the sudden dawn and a donkey braying at first light. Staying in bed feels like a waste of time. Drowsiness will come later in the day—after the lunchtime pina colada which is followed by a siesta in preparation for sundown festivities. For the sun sinks early in the tropics. The home-owner still has the garden to attend to, with its rampaging growth after a tropical rainstorm and fencing to be maintained against the monkeys and goats. But the pace is leisurely and activities generally have to be invented if needed at all. For excited visitors enjoying their first taste of the tropics, magic lies everywhere—in the landscape, the ocean, the mountain.

Ah, yes, the mountain. It is easy to forget from high ground that there is a higher summit above, a peak covered in forest, the home of echoing birds, of dripping waters and of trees thrusting their way through the jungle to reach the sunlight. It is the rain forest essential to the island's water supply, sourced by the clouds' attraction to the mountain peak and the constant dampness which trickles down the slope. Nature has worked it out. It is why thick foliage grows on this island while the flat islands can go for rainless months and rely on the rainy season not to let them down. The mountain, too thick in places to be explored, holds irresistible secrets. Just to look up at the harmless clouds anchored around the peak was to wonder how to get up there, to feel the freshness amid the warmth, to see from there the uninterrupted view of the ocean and the land lying at one's feet. It must be the ambition of everyone who visits the island to climb the mountain, not just to enjoy the intoxicating menu of Caribbean activities but because, as the mountaineer would say: 'because it's there'.

Alison and Ryan were as transfixed by the scenery as anyone else visiting for the first time. The plants and the views, the relaxed island ways, the sounds and the smells and the wrap-around warmth of a new climate, all of these new experiences would fill them with awe, but nothing more than the sleepy mountain and its smile of gentle persuasion beckoning them to investigate its mysteries. Bob could give them the lowdown on how to climb it.

"It's a gentle climb, not dangerous, but you have to watch where you're going. There is only one route up, an old water course. It gets steeper further up and that part is a bit challenging. The only real obstacle is crossing the ravine: there is a rope bridge and you have to hang on to the sides, but it's not difficult in daylight. You won't suffer vertigo much because the tall trees in the ravine rise till they almost reach the bridge so if you look down you can only see the canopy of the trees a few feet below you. If anyone was unlucky enough to fall off the bridge they would fall through the canopy and that would be curtains, but you would have to be careless for that to happen. There is of course no mountain rescue team here, so once you've landed in the jungle from a great height that's where you'd stay!" "How often do you climb the mountain?" Alison asked. "Good heavens, not any more" Bob shrugged. "I used to do it regularly when I was young. It's a doddle for someone of your age but not for me. My balance is not as good as it used to be and I wouldn't trust myself on the rope bridge now. Besides, the climb is too steep, and I have done it so often I don't need to prove myself any more. But it gives one a sense of achievement the first few times. If you want to climb it I can show you where to start and then you just follow the water course to the top. It's about three hours up and one and a half down... a nice half-day expedition. It will knock you out for the afternoon and you will feel a huge sense of satisfaction at drinks time in the evening."

It was the third morning of their holiday when Alison and Ryan set out for the climb after breakfast on the balcony with Bob and the attendant Vincent. They had waited for a clear day when the top of the mountain was free from cloud, at least from all but a few puffs which moved slowly past it and vanished across the sea. The weather was settled, as predicted. Conditions for a simple climb were ideal. All they needed to bring were light rucksacks, water bottles and some sandwiches with which to celebrate their arrival at the peak. A tea-shirt, shorts and trainers would suffice for the walk.

They crossed the grassy hillside, past wild orange trees and a pond thick with dragonflies and water lilies and easily found the gap in the trees which marked the entrance to the rain forest. A well-worn undulating path took them through shaded plants still light green from the sun's energy until the forest started to darken and the sunshine was reduced to a filter. The trees became taller and straighter. They were now on a bare pathway and heading upwards on a gentle slope which became gradually more uneven as the route steepened. Roots spread across their track making it necessary to hang on to a branch or hanging vine to avoid getting a foot caught in the space beneath. But Bob had been right: it was a simple challenge for young people like them. Just look where they were going and the route would present no problems.

The rope bridge appeared without warning. They had hardly noticed the ravine ahead, so clear and hazard-free was the water course on which they travelled. With due care, they followed the centre of the bridge gripping the ropes at waist level on either side. The tree canopy beneath them was reassuring though they were mindful of the gulf below. Maybe it would have been better not to have known about the depth of the ravine. On the other hand it made them more cautious, more careful to walk in the middle of the platform. The bridge sagged and swayed a little but without cause for alarm. It only took a minute to cross. 'Not a problem' they smiled to each other with a tinge of relief as they stepped on to firm ground again.

From now on the climb became still steeper. The higher they went the damper and more slippery it became. They started to feel the coolness of the air, warmed as they were by their exertions. The tree roots which at a lower level had been an obstruction now helped with pulling themselves up as their footholds slithered from under them. They clung on to bare branches of spindly trees heaving themselves up stage by stage, their trainers now mud-soaked and their shorts blackened by the volcanic earth. The final scramble towards the summit was hard going but the prospect of reaching the top was the irresistible prize. Suddenly the bush parted in front of them, the ground flattened and they broke through on to the summit, into the open air, cloud swirling around them in an unexpected chill. Intermittent views of the land below showed them how high they had climbed. A chain of islands stretching in line till visibility vanished into the haze gave them a perspective that they could never have imagined.

—

Shifting their position along the narrow ridge they found a rock on which to catch their breath. Surprised by the comparative ease of the climb they felt the thrill of achievement and the satisfaction of having done something nobody at home would ever have done. They had completed the climb in considerably less time than the predicted three hours. At their age they could work miracles, they could probably break the record for the descent as well. In fact they might claim the record for the entire up-and-down exercise, except that there probably was no known record to beat. They could sit on their rock, admire the scenery, cool off with a bottle of water, munch a sandwich and lose themselves in the silence and beauty of the view.

Away from the cares of a complicated world the mind has room for invention. Caution makes way for heroic thoughts. To gaze ahead to the opposite side of the mountain, to the dotted villages and patchy farms lying far below in the sunshine, would be enough to inspire a sense of adventure in many people. In a young, fit and competitive couple it could well tempt an ambitious move: uncertain, but exciting and original. Bob had not mentioned descending the other side of the mountain, a straight-over-the-top excursion. This might be the only occasion they had to show him how it was done. The idea developed quickly and thrillingly in Alison and Ryan. It might take a little longer down the other side, but time was not a factor. They would go for it.

The thin shrub presented few problems as they started their descent. It seemed a simple exercise at first but the rainforest became thicker as the scrub prospered on the rich volcanic soil. There was no path to lead them and the couple had to rely on their sense of direction. So long as they were going downhill, that was what mattered. The bush was getting thicker. Small trees mingled with bamboo to form an almost impenetrable barrier. Progress became pitifully slow and the timelessness they had felt at the summit was developing into urgency. It was decision time either to turn back and climb again up through the stinging bush or to go on. The thought of finding themselves back at the top late in the day and then having to negotiate the tree roots on the muddy water course once more did not appeal. Added to that, crossing the rope bridge in the failing light would not be advisable. Surely the bush would dissolve the further they descended and they would be out on to grassland before the sun went down. They continued downwards.

As the sky darkened and their rate of descent became almost static, realisation crept in that they would not reach the end of their chancy excursion before nightfall. They thought of poor Uncle Bob who would be worrying about them and feeling responsible for their well-being. Happily it was a clear night and no rain cloud touched the mountain though tee-shirt and shorts were utterly inadequate clothing for a night out in the bush. But they had each other's embrace for warmth. Their remaining sandwich and what water they had left would sustain them till morning. The next few hours were going to be a test of endurance. The altitude was still too high for sand flies: their enemies until now had been the increasing presence of spikes from thorn-bush which had scratched and torn at their clothes. Now they feared they could come under night attack from spiders, poisonous insects or unknown creatures of the forest. But somehow they would survive—get through this one night of discomfort. A new day would surely lift their spirits and enable them to proceed downwards to hope and security.

—

At the first sign of light filtering through the tall bush they struck out, fighting their way forwards, downwards, valuing every step of progress as a move towards safety. They thought again about the anxiety Uncle Bob must be feeling and of their own irresponsibility in placing him in such a difficult position. Determination pushed them on through the jungle, squeezing them between the trunks of hardwood tree and shrub, scraping them through the smallest gap which lowered them slowly towards safety. As the vegetation started to thin out their rate of progress quickened, very slightly, but increasingly and noticeably. The trees themselves seemed to be getting less hostile, more cultured, more sympathetic to human existence; shafts of light shot like laser-beams more frequently through the branches. Suddenly there appeared a patch of brown earth, maybe a path, an entrance to the jungle—or to them, pray God, an exit. A blaze of sunlight hit them. Exhausted they emerged through the last soft leaves of the forest and felt the grassland under their feet. As the breeze hit them, the blue sky opened above. They had made it.

———

"What are you telling me, Vincent?" Bob asked, shocked by Vincent's words. "Are you saying that you haven't seen them all day? That they went out after breakfast and never returned? Someone must have seen them in town or down on the beach. Where they hell are they? Have you looked in their room?"

"I look everywhere," Vincent replied, "and I sure they not return today."

"Perhaps they came back and then went out again when I was having my siesta."

"No, they not come back. I ask in the village, has anyone seen them come down? No one has."

"Did they tell you what time they would be getting back?"

"No, they say something about seeing how quick they could get to the top and I tell them do not take risks. They promise they take care and they go off with some sandwiches I make. I sure they be a' right. They love it here."

"That's what worries me. They love it so much they will take it for granted and do something stupid: go swimming on a dangerous beach or something."

"I certain they not go swimming. They excited by the mountain. I sure they be up there still."

"That's what I fear" said Bob. "They must be up there still," he repeated thoughtfully. "It's too late to raise a search party now. The police won't do anything till the morning."

There was a pause in the conversation as the grim possibility of a serious accident to the young couple gripped the two men. There were few options. They were resigned to the action they had to take. To wait for morning and leave Alison and Ryan there on the mountain was unthinkable. They would go up to the mountain now, instantly. They would follow the regular track. Whatever it took, they would find them.

Grabbing such torches and flashlights as they could find, low batteries notwithstanding, the two men set out in the twilight. The settled weather meant that the sky still held some brightness, enough for them to see their way confidently across the meadow on the hillside, where herdsmen were still bringing in their cattle, until they found the well-used gap in the bushes and entered the rain forest, their hearts beating fast. In the darkness the frail light from the torches could just make out the route but it took all their concentration to keep on the right path. They had just one mission, to find Alison and Ryan. Their minds would be on nothing else.

—

Alison and Ryan collapsed on the firm ground, not knowing where they were. Their relief at having survived at all far outweighed any concern but as they recovered their senses they understood gradually how far they were from home. It would take hours to walk it. But first they must find the road. They knew that there was only one main road which girthed the island. By walking downhill they were bound to find it and then get their bearings for the way home. They staggered on down over the lower slope of the mountain, pushed through a straggly hedge, jumped a dry ditch and stumbled on to the road. The heat of the sun on the grit road would hinder their journey home.

For long minutes they walked in silence, careful to preserve their energy. But then they heard a welcome noise: it was the sound of a vehicle approaching them from behind, scuffing the road and throwing up dust as they looked back. They were about to flag it down when they noticed it slowing. It drew alongside them and stopped. With hope rising they gazed vaguely at the taxi as though it were a mirage. They were just aware of a voice summoning them in friendly tones... a voice they recognised from somewhere. "Hello," called the driver, "Remember me? Mayhew ... remember? I took you to the village when you arrived. What in Lord's name are you two doing here? Get in. You look like you had a rough time." Mayhew, the saviour. Yes, of course they remembered him. As they bumped slowly along the road they were just able to describe their ordeal. He listened in silence. Then he made his statement. "My God, man." he exploded. "Why the hell you do that? There ain't no track down the mountain this side. Oh, dear Jesus, oh, no, no. No man go that way. You both lucky to escape. The mountain hold a lot of trickery, oh, yes, it play a lot of tricks. I just hear on the radio the police has sent out a search team to look for missing persons." He paused while they all digested what he had said. Then Alison said, "They've turned out to look for us. That's so good of them but …Oh, Lord, think of the trouble we've caused. Can we stop at the police station, Mayhew, to let them know we're safe? We have to tell them at once." "Sure thing," said Mayhew, "but they say on the radio how they were looking for two men." "Well, they got that part wrong," said Ryan, "did they mention any names?" "No, they not give any names. They just say two men." "The media often get things wrong," said Alison. "Could be," said Mayhew doubtfully, "but local radio hear it direct from the police, and the police hear it from herdsmen, the radio say. Herdsmen have keen eyes. They not get it wrong.

They tell police they see two men with torches enter the forest after sunset. The house cleaner reported them missing this morning." He paused. "So you needn't worry. The police team won't be looking for you."

Reassuring as Mayhew's words were intended to be, a sense of unease was creeping into the couple in the back of the car. As Mayhew drove up the twin strips of concrete through the village to the big house above, Alison and Ryan could not help feeling troubled by what Mayhew had told them.

"Any new report? Have they been found yet?" Mayhew had stopped his car on the hill and shouted to a village dweller.

"No, man… no sign of them. It's a terrible, terrible business," came the reply. "The police say all they find as yet is a torch with a flat battery lying on the bridge."

The Rabbit Run

Arthur Wallace stared out of the window as the train sped through lifeless swathes of countryside. Scrubland, embankment, disused industrial sites, thickets, woodland and flat open spaces—all useful in their own way, he thought, so long as he could find them again.

He was searching for a site so undesirable, so unusable, so barren that nobody, no person of any interest or occupation, would have occasion to visit it. At the same time, it had to be somewhere he himself could reach. There must be plenty of land in this country, Mr Wallace pondered, that nobody ever trod, year in year out, places on which no dog walker, no rambler, no birdwatcher, no maintenance worker had set foot from time immemorial, ground so totally worthless as to lie untouched by human presence till time without end.

Mr Wallace believed from his carriage window that he could identify several such sites. He would have to remember their location by reference to landmarks visible from the train, distances from a distinctive tree, stream or derelict building, the time measured from the last station to a point at which a frequented area had long since melted into a nondescript and deserted landscape. And yet, of course, it had to be accessible to Mr Wallace. That would be the trick, finding a site desolate enough to be ignored by humans but which could be reached on foot by a middle-aged man, carrying a heavy load, unnoticed.

It is generally assumed in the criminal world that the search for a missing person will begin in the back garden of their last known address. People of no known identity can sometimes vanish without attracting attention or fade from the memory in the belief that they had moved to another part of the country—missing persons who would never be missed. Whether the body which Mr Wallace had on his premises answered that description was debatable but the burial-in-the-back-garden option was a risk Mr Wallace was not prepared to take.

His erstwhile housemate, Eric, had been a vagrant ever since his drunken father kicked him out of their home when he was still in his teens. He had attempted to find a job but, having no training for such a thing, resorted to drugs, wandering the streets, finding unused doorways to sleep in, begging or stealing whatever he could get and unable to register any ambition, or to extricate himself from his hopeless routine.

Mr. Wallace found Eric one morning lying in a sleeping-bag outside his garage. A respectable, detached house in a suburban street it was, with a well-kept lawn in front and a concrete slope to the garage beside it. Under the stewardship of the fastidious Mr Wallace it had developed into an ideal bachelor residence, suited to a single person who lived without need for society—to a loner, in fact, such as Mr Wallace had become. A mild-mannered and unassuming man, he would have enjoyed the company of others had he had the confidence to make friends, but he remained a private person, safe in his anonymity, unnoticed by his neighbours.

Eric had found seclusion in the garage entrance and Mr Wallace, taking pity on him had invited him inside his house for a warm drink and a moment of comfort. It was intended as a short-term arrangement but it is a well-established fact that temporary measures soon take on a permanency unless terminated early on. Eric needed some friendship, some security. He could do with the guidance of a fatherly figure. Most of all he needed somewhere to settle while he straightened out his aimless life. Mr Wallace too was happy to find companionship. To provide Eric with safe lodging and stability satisfied his repressed need to achieve something for the community by helping a lost soul to find the meaning of life for the first time. So Eric stayed on.

At first the two men got on well enough together enjoying the company which each had lacked in his own life, but once the novelty started to wear off, they began to realise that they had little in common, few mutual interests to discuss and an entirely different set of domestic standards. One of the only thrills they could share was a visit to the local town football club on drab Saturday afternoons to sit anonymously among the few hundred spectators and watch their wretched team grind out a typical goalless draw. Eric would often stay in bed till after ten in the morning while his host tidied up the house. He made no financial contribution and, worse still, no attempt to find a job, while Mr Wallace paid the bills without any show of thanks from his feckless lodger. Eric's lack of initiative started to become a drag on Mr Wallace's finances and a daily test of his goodwill. Eric was seen as a sponger, a burden on his host's hospitality which could drag on indefinitely unless the unavoidable truth was tackled head on. As Mr Wallace grew more restless, frustrated by the failure of his experiment, he resolved to tell Eric of his decision. Eric's occupation of Mr Wallace's home had to end. Giving notice was not something which came naturally to Mr Wallace but it could no longer be avoided.

Reasonable and understanding as he was, Mr Wallace did his best to explain his situation to Eric, who met his request to leave the house with blank unconcern. Eric was staying put. He had no other option and was content to remain as he was. Mr Wallace found himself trapped. Arguments became more heated and Eric's complacency intolerable— until one day without warning Mr Wallace's patience snapped. In a fury of frustration, he struck Eric with his fist as hard as he could. Eric went down like a sack of coal. He never uttered again. Intentional or not, this unplanned act, quite out of character for such a gentle soul as Mr Wallace, landed him in an unimaginable crisis. He now had a body on his hands.

A horrified Mr Wallace was suddenly shaken from his quiet life. Mild of character he may have been but his solitary existence had developed an independence in him and an inner strength to deal with unexpected events without panic. He held his nerve and, as the hours passed, he started to rehearse his options. Should he go to the police? It would not look good to admit that he alone had been responsible for Eric's death, after initially inviting him into his home. There would have to be a trial. He could expect a long prison sentence even if he were able to establish manslaughter in place of murder, which was by no means certain. On the other hand, such was Eric's anonymity that surely none of Mr Wallace's neighbours, nor anyone else for that matter, would have noticed his disappearance. One day he might just find his way on to the missing person's list, but even that was unlikely for a floater like Eric.

And so it was that one afternoon Mr Wallace slipped his car unnoticed out of the garage, to drive north to a site in the deep countryside his train journey had identified, Eric's body secured in industrial sacks in the boot. He was heading for a place so remote it had taken hours to plot the itinerary, the time of arrival, the method of disposal and the exit strategy, so as to depart the scene secure in the knowledge that he had left no tracks, no suspicions and no anxieties behind him. It would be an ordeal but once safely home, he could return his life to its normal obscurity and forget about Eric and the whole unhappy event.

For four hours he drove along the motorway, before turning off for a further hour—far, far out into a wilderness of heathland and ancient pines. Down a straight, traffic-less road he drove, past a ruined cottage and then turned off on to a barely passable track, before guiding his car on to a grass bank, pine trees overhanging, rough bushes obscuring the place from all directions. The light was fading, as anticipated. The air was filled by a sinister silence. Mr Wallace dragged Eric's body out of the boot of the car and heaved it on to his back. Anywhere within an impenetrable thicket would do. It was obvious that no one ever came this way. A convenient rabbit track made things easier for carrying a body further, still further, into the unknown. Mr Wallace pushed his way through long grasses, brambles tugging at his trousers, angry nettles witnessing the poverty of the land. A few strides into the jungle off the rabbit track saw Mr Wallace poised to deposit the body. He made sure it would not be caught up in any brambles. He let the black sacks fall through the undergrowth into a dip in the ground, checked they were completely hidden from land or air and set about extracting himself from the oppressive thickness of the featureless landscape. The only sound was the rumble of a distant train.

The way back was challenging. Mr Wallace was loath to carry a torch, but sufficient natural light allowed him to reach his car. Things had gone to plan. A relieved Mr Wallace was congratulating himself when something caught his eye. Further down the track there appeared to be a figure standing. He could just make it out in the fading light: it was a person, motionless. Mr Wallace knew he must remain calm. He would get into his car and drive back down the track towards the figure, behaving as normally as he could. As Mr Wallace's car approached, the figure remained standing in the middle of the track. He held a shotgun under his arm. A springer spaniel sat beside him.

"Can I help you at all", said the man peering through the driver's window, "you look lost?"

"No, I'm OK, thanks" said Mr Wallace, "I just had to pull off the road. I've had a long journey and I still have a way to go."

"I can see from your number plate that you aren't local. I'm the ranger for this area and I saw you turn into this track earlier. Forgive my asking, but you were a long time up there. Is everything all right?"

"Not quite," said Mr Wallace, thinking fast, "I dropped a credit card which I must have pulled out of my pocket when I had a pee. I was looking for it."

"I am sure we can help," said the ranger. "Russet here will find it for you. Won't you, Russ?... She'll find anything, my dog will. Just show me roughly where you were, sir."

After a few uneasy minutes helping them search for something he knew didn't exist, Mr Wallace said, "Let's not worry. I'll have the card stopped. It's better than spending time looking for it now." "Of course," replied the ranger, "but I'll be this way tomorrow anyhow, and it will give Russ something to do. She's got a wonderful nose, has Russ. She'll pick up any scent. Only last week she tracked a wounded deer half a mile away and led me to it. It doesn't matter how thick the brambles are, she slips under them like an eel." The ranger took a notebook from his top pocket. "When we find it in the morning I'll mail it to you. Give me your details and I'll send it on?"

"No, really, don't worry," said Mr Wallace, "I'll stop the card," adding hurriedly, "I must get going or I'll be late but thank you." Mr Wallace got back in his car and drove slowly, with a deepening sense of unease, down the track to the road. The ranger stood in mid-track staring after him, curious—and wondering why the car had turned on to the road heading back the way it had come.

Briar Cottage

"I've got a great idea," said Steve, breaking the silence. "What is it?" muttered his wife Emma in a detached sort of way without looking up from her book. "I've thought of a terrific idea for our next party," Steve went on. Emma started, this time looking up in shock, "Oh, no, for heaven's sake, surely not, "she said, "not after the complete hash you made of the last one, making your guests drive around the county searching hopelessly for things in locked churches and names on gravestones which didn't exist. Surely you're not thinking of giving another party. I don't think I could bear another catastrophe like that one." "No, it won't be like that one, not this time," Steve tried to remain calm and reassuring. "This one will be closer to home: no cars involved, it will happen within a short distance from here. All of the action will be on foot. People will love it because it will be something entirely different and it will be really stimulating. It will be our own kind of mystery thriller. There are companies which organise events like this, where you have to guess who committed some crime or other, and they are tremendously popular. The whole world likes a mystery." Emma continued to look horrified, "You mentioned a word there," she said, "rather a key word which you have failed to grasp. That word is 'organise' and, if your idea, whatever it is, needs any degree of organising then I'd advise you to drop it. You're fine with a straightforward party with plenty to drink and me to do the food but organisation is not your strong suit." She looked down at her book again and her voice trailed away, "just forget it. It's not worth all the upset you caused our friends last time. I still feel embarrassed about it." She read on.

This discouraging put-down might have concluded the argument in the eyes of most people, but Steve did not see it that way. He was sure of his ground.

His was such a cracking-good idea he had to go along with it: it was thrilling and, best of all, original. He doubted if it had ever been tried before because such an opportunity as this seldom presented itself. It would be a shame to ignore the chance. He could imagine how his friends would look back on the occasion and laugh about it years later remembering that night they all met at the deserted cottage.

The cottage in question stood on the edge of Tyrrell's Wood, up the road from where Steve and Emma lived. The couple's home was remote enough, set amid fertile pastures half a mile outside a rural hamlet, while the cottage, which had grabbed Steve's imagination, was a short walk further on, tucked away down a green lane, accessible only on foot. The lane now was seldom used and had become darkened by hedgerows hanging with wild bush and brambles. Not for nothing was the little house beside the wood known as Briar Cottage. It had belonged to Steve's family for three generations and had been occupied by a woodman and his family countless years before who, according to rumour, had suddenly left for no apparent reason and had vanished without telling their employers. Since it had no running water, electricity or any other services it was uninhabitable thereafter and had remained unoccupied save by small woodland creatures and roof-nesting birds. Considering its state of abandonment the cottage had not suffered from neglect as much as one would expect and with a sound roof had stayed mainly dry and resistant to the elements, being too remote to attract the attention of vandals. In short it was just the place for a good party, so long as Steve could invent a motive and let his mind wander into the fresh fields of his imagination.

"All right," said Emma, looking up at last after an uneasy silence, "what is this mad idea of yours? If it's as simple as you make out, you might get away with it. If it's not, I don't want to know." "I promise you," Steve replied "it will be a fantastic adventure which will be talked about for years. If you'll listen for an instant I will tell you what I have in mind, then you might get the message. It's like this: you know Briar Cottage in the green lane which has been unoccupied for years—not since the woodman left before I was born? Well, it's still in fairly good shape in spite of having been neglected for so long. The lane is overgrown and the cottage itself is pretty lonely standing there beside the wood, but that is all part of the plan. I could conjure up a story about it, a sort of mystery and we could visit it as it got dark and I could create a bit of atmosphere and we could look for something there." "Oh, no, surely not another treasure hunt," said Emma horrified, "what on earth would you look for anyway? There's nothing there." "That's the point," Steve shot back, "you're right. There is nothing there. But I'm going to pretend there is something or, better still, there may be something there that nobody knows about. And I am going to make sure of it by arranging for something – or someone – to be there. Someone who will appear when they least expect it. I shall have the help of an accomplice who is good for a laugh." "Do you mean you will go to the cottage in a group and then one of your crazy friends will jump out and scare the life out of them? That's really corny. I thought you said yours was an original idea." "No, dear," replied Steve patiently, "No, it won't be like that. I have prepared a story that will fascinate them, just a bit of mystery to keep them guessing. For a start, they will all be wondering why I hadn't invited Arnold for the evening. Arnold's at every party and they'll miss him at once. I'll create an excuse about his being delayed and I'll tell the guests he will be joining us later… and he will in fact join us, but not quite where they expect him. You know what a character he is, game for anything, including this one: suddenly appearing in a top room in the cottage. He's a real actor, he'll be hilarious."

"I hope Arnold knows what he's letting himself in for," said Emma anxiously. "Have you cleared it with him?" "Not yet," said Steve, "but he knows the gist of it… he knows there's no electricity at the cottage, no mobile signal and all that. I'll be giving him full details about the cottage, its history as a woodman's house, the way it was cleared of all contents when the woodman left and the upstairs room where I want Arnold to wait for the party to arrive. He'll have a comfortable folding chair and a book to read while waiting for them to appear and a strong torch to read by. I shall personally show him up the staircase to the room where he will wait for us all to arrive. The front window will be closed so as not to give the game away but the rear window of the room will be open on the woodland side. He will have everything he needs but he won't be alone for long anyway. I've already told him about my idea and he likes it. He has said that as long as he doesn't have to wait long in a completely empty house, he's happy. Arnold is a real sport, he likes a challenge."

"And what's this story you are going to tell your guests?" Emma enquired. "What will they be expecting?" "That's the exciting part of it", said Steve, "When everyone is here, I am going to spend a few minutes telling them about the deserted cottage in the woods to fire their imaginations, how many years it has been locked up and kept empty. I shall explain about the woodman leaving unexpectedly, without telling his employers, and then... and this will be the mystery that they will all love—I shall mention that there is just one room upstairs in the house which was always locked and has never been entered. Then I shall tell them that I have found a spare key which I think will fit the lock. The purpose of our visit will be to enter the room where we think the woodman slept and see what's inside. That will really make them sit up." Steve paused to see what effect it had on Emma, who was looking even more doubtful than before. "Of course, the only thing inside the room will be Arnold shining his torch. And you can bet he will play his role as spookily as he can. Think what their reaction will be when they break into the room and find a figure inside... and then, when they are really hyped up, they'll realise it's Arnold... and it was all a hoax! It's a real cracker, this idea. I wonder why nobody has thought of it before!"

Emma's attitude did not entirely accord with Steve's enthusiasm. She was anxious about a lot of things: what if it rained, for instance; the clothing the party would need; or the condition of the rough ground in the lane in the dark and a thousand and one other things that would have to be taken into account. She was also less than comfortable with the effect it might have on a nervous guest without warning finding a person in the room, lit only by the light of a torch. But above all she was worried about Steve's ability to manage such an adventure, it still sounded like another of his impulsive schemes. It was a big risk but on reflection a better option than a chaotic treasure hunt in cars like his last disaster. At least she would organise the party herself when they returned from the cottage, so the evening would not be a complete flop.

Arnold had his own reservations about the scheme but his sporting attitude took over. He had half committed himself and would go through with it. He was suspicious about Steve's track record for organising events but he would not let a good friend down. He would find himself a book to read, wait for the party to appear and use his torch at the last minute to indicate a presence in the room. There would be no need to scare anyone, just to create a sense of mystery to tie in with the story that Steve will have told the group. He had not worked out what he would do when the group reached the cottage. There is no rehearsal for this kind of entertainment. It's the spontaneity that makes it fun.

Arnold, with his own props for the exciting evening ahead, walked with Steve along the country road which led to the green lane. It was a relief to know that the weather was fine. It had not rained for several days, there was a light breeze and conditions were dry underfoot. Out here in the depth of the country there was no man-made sound to disturb the silence of the evening. Entering the lane Arnold noticed a remarkable stillness giving him a sense of increasing isolation as he and Steve approached the cottage. The grass path deadened the sound of their footsteps. The fading light blended the cottage into the tall trees which packed themselves around it. Arnold consoled himself by calculating that Steve and Emma's guests would be arriving very soon back at their house. They would be met by Emma and would shortly after that be joined by Steve. Then the evening would begin, and he, Arnold, would soon afterwards be playing his role for the unsuspecting group approaching the cottage and the mystery it held.

Steve opened the door to the cottage, shone a torch at the empty passageway and felt his way across the stone floor to the bottom of the staircase leading to the upper room. Arnold followed him up the stairs. Steve paused on the landing outside the room and felt for the door handle. The door swung slowly on its rusty hinges and the two men stumbled inside. The room was bare, as Steve already knew, but there was a definite musty smell and a strange atmosphere about the room which was both unwelcoming and oppressive. Opening a window on the woodland side improved the quality of the air but did nothing to reduce the feeling that all was not well. Had something happened in the room to give it such an unhappy atmosphere? It was consoling for Arnold that he would not be occupying it for long. Indeed, the sooner Steve left to meet his guests, the sooner they would be back. Steve made sure that Arnold had his book, his torch for reading and all he needed for his short wait, and with some reassuring words made his way out of the cottage for his ten-minute walk back home to greet his guests.

"They're nearly all here, "Emma announced as Steve returned, breathless in anticipation of the evening's adventure. "Everyone's arrived, except for Rosie and Giles. They called a few minutes ago to say they had been held up by an incident in Houndsmere but would get here as soon as they could. They shouldn't be more than 15 minutes or so."

"That's not good news, "said Steve, "I promised Arnold we would be at the cottage as soon as we could and I don't want to leave him there long. It will be uncomfortable for him waiting there on his own. I'll gather the guests around now, describe the reason for them being here, tell them about the deserted cottage and the un-entered room and gee them up a bit with a sense of mystery. By the time I have finished Rosie and Giles will be here and we can get moving. I'll give them an extra five minutes at the end, if necessary, because I don't want them to miss the fun."

As he heard the front door of the cottage close downstairs, an intense feeling of abandonment came over Arnold. He could picture Steve setting off back to his home, noiselessly along the green lane. Steve would return but already he knew that the intervening minutes would be long. He was worried that they might feel interminable. He felt a loneliness he had never experienced before. He shone his torch around the room but there was no one there, as he well knew, except that he sensed someone else's presence. That musty smell seemed to have got stronger. The heavy atmosphere in the room was competing with the silence. He had a sense that he was intruding, that he had no right to be there. Arnold went to the window which looked out into the wood, but the only sound was of a hushed breeze ruffling the undergrowth and the clicking of branches from the tall trees. It was the emptiness of that silence which disturbed him most. He wondered what had induced him to place himself in this position. Arnold tried to cast aside his anxieties. Maybe he was more sensitive than he had expected. He would simply sit on his stool, train his torch on his book and lose himself in its pages. Steve and his friends would be back before he knew it.

Yet, as he read, he found he could not concentrate on the meaning of the words. His surroundings were dominating his thoughts. He heard a sound outside of a branch snapping as though someone had trodden on it but it must have been an animal. There were plenty of nocturnal animals in the woods, he told himself, and noises at nightfall would also be made by birds on their hunting expeditions. He tried reading his book again but his imagination wandered in response to each sound outside. Another twig cracked. Surely animals are too sure-footed to tread on loose branches, aren't they? Yet it must have been an animal. No person would wander in a wood at this hour. Ten minutes had passed. Steve would be meeting his guests. It would be a long time before they would set out. But Arnold was not inclined to leave the room. He was more fearful of what he might face outside it. It was safer to remain inside, he thought, uncomfortable as it felt. He tried to settle with his book again but could not resist wayward thoughts: that Steve may not have fastened the front door securely, or what might be lurking in the other rooms in the cottage, or why the woodman had left in such a hurry all those years ago, leaving the cottage unoccupied for all that time. Maybe even Steve didn't know, or maybe he'd never investigated. All Steve could tell him was that the cottage had been cleared and was empty of all contents. The only item in the place was the stool Arnold was sitting on. There came another sound, this time closer to the cottage, a sound like a thump, a deliberate but muffled blow, an animal perhaps kicking at a tree stump…though it would have to be a large animal. It had to be a deer, Arnold told himself, but a big one to make such an impact on a tree. The woods fell silent again, save for the breeze which rattled his open window very slightly. Through the blurred words of his book Arnold heard the window hinge creak, at least he assumed it was his window creaking. Or had it come from another part of the cottage? It was the very faintest creak, but enough to make Arnold's heart thump loudly. A creaking hinge can only mean one thing, that something is opening or closing. It cannot be the front door since Steve must have closed it firmly when he left. It must have been the window in his room. Arnold had to convince himself that it was. He had to be assured. He listened for the next breeze to repeat it. Minutes passed, long, anxious minutes. But the breeze refused to rattle the window and its hinges failed to creak. Arnold was standing gazing at the wall, fighting for his composure. Then came another sound, a sound from inside the house more sinister than any. It was the sharp tread, as Arnold heard it, the stamp of a footstep on the stair, an interval of a few seconds and then another one. Somebody was coming up the staircase, slowly and deliberately, up to the room. Arnold stood there frozen. He was certain there was someone standing on the landing right outside the room. Arnold could feel the power of their presence. Should he cry out? Or should he stay quiet, hoping the intruder would leave? Or should he hold the door handle so that anyone trying to enter would feel resistance and believe the door was locked? His mind was scrambled. Blind terror overtook him. He…

"I'm sorry we were delayed," said Giles when he and Rosie at last arrived. "I hope it hasn't held you up." "Well, we gave you a few extra minutes," Steve replied impatiently, "and we are running late, so we'll get off now and I'll explain our mystery to you as we walk along. I am not sure what we are going to find but I am sure it will be interesting when we get there." Steve smirked.

The group filed into the green lane and, with Steve at the head, made their way along the grass track, spurred by the thrill of adventure. Steve had inspired them with spooky anticipation at what mystery the upstairs room would reveal. Shortly they would arrive at the deserted cottage and one or two of them would volunteer to mount the staircase and be the first people in years to enter the forbidden room. Then they would all enjoy unravelling the mystery, feel the thrill of being in this ghostly place and then go back to Emma's delicious meal and leave Steve to pour the wine. To heighten the atmosphere Steve made the group keep silence. They would approach the cottage stealthily and without talking. They were nearing the cottage now.

Suddenly a shout caught the evening air, then another shout. But they were not shouts of welcome, that was obvious. Steve heard them with instant alarm. He stopped dead and held out his arm to restrain the others. As they listened, they heard the muffled noise of a desperate scream coming from the cottage. It was the male voice of someone in deep distress. Was this what they had come for, some of the group wondered? Steve stared in horror, then shouted to Giles and together they ran in panic towards the cottage. Steve flung open the door and they fled up the staircase and into the room. Arnold's torch was shining, his stool was in place. Arnold was lying collapsed in a corner of the room.

—

"You will have to help yourselves tonight," said Emma in disgust, "I am off to see Arnold. He is severely traumatised and they will be keeping him in for observation for the night. What a bloody crazy scheme that was! God knows what gets into some people," (making it plain from the direction of her glance who that 'some people' was) "I just hope Arnold gets over this quickly, I can think of a lot of people who would be scarred for life by an experience like this."

Steve was pouring the drinks in a subdued manner, deflated and embarrassed by the anticlimactic events of the evening. "I never thought it would have that effect on a strong person like Arnold," he said, "I should never have asked him to do it but he seemed so right for the occasion. I shall apologise to him as soon as they discharge him tomorrow. I just didn't believe that anything could go wrong. He was safe in the house and there was nobody who could possibly harm him there."

"I am sure you are right," Giles replied. "no harm could ever have come to him in that cottage. All the same I think you should get rid of that rusty old axe someone has left on the landing."

Hotel Imperius

It would be hard to find two better friends than Tom and Bertram. They had missed the rivalry that bedevils one's early schooldays and met for the first time only when their university days began. By that time maturity in most young adults has developed a tolerance of one's fellow citizens whom one has learnt to appreciate, and to admire for their differences and latent abilities. Competitiveness becomes less important and friendships are built on the basis of shared interests, a fascination for the talents of colleagues and the satisfaction of enjoying activities with them. Thus the relationship between

Tom Curtis and Bertram McAdam was unhindered by a struggle for supremacy or envy for some mundane honour on the sports field. They had also avoided having to compete against each other for top place in the form, or bottom place if that was more appropriate. Neither of them had had to take his position in the front row on sports day to collect an award for virtue while the other sat at the back scowling and resentful. They had in effect come to higher education together by separate routes with a clear run to forming a friendship which would be expected to endure throughout their adult lives.

Their rooms at college were in the same corridor, they both studied modern languages and they shared interests in the outdoor life, cycling, keeping fit, weekend tennis and boating on the river. They enjoyed literature, played chess and had a cursory connection with amateur dramatics. Being well-balanced individuals they went drinking with their friends in a modest way, telling anecdotes, inspiring light conversation, laughter and lively debate. They joined in with the society that the university offered, contributing to a range of activities that covered the academic, athletic and social in equal measure. Without excelling at any one thing or driving any of their colleagues to feeling inferior because of their successes they skated along through their university careers with a stress-less serenity which many would doubtless have envied, if envy had ever been part of their agenda.

After they had graduated they spent time together, sometimes back-packing across the stony landscapes of Greek islands or joining similarly carefree groups of travellers on safari in southern Africa. At this point they had not yet got down to the hard realities of an existence independent of parents. They had not savoured the responsibilities of competing for a living in a world of hard truths—of settling into a career in which dull routine would challenge the character and individuality of each of them. These intervening months on coming down from university were spent in thrills, adventures and travel. They only needed a shoestring to get by. Everything was initiative, risk and invention, communing with local people and using their experience of modern languages to make friends and visit them in their homes. The sun mostly seemed to shine, the hot climates relaxed them and days passed to a background of silent hills and walks along trails that sheep had made. It was ideal for anyone without a care in the world. But the world has never provided that for ever. The days of reality would come soon enough. And soon enough they did.

The noise of city traffic on the way to work found Tom in subdued form, mindful of his office duties, a formal attitude framing his day. Desk-work in a partitioned bay, separated from the sound of his colleague in the space next to him, was his routine, his daily condition of work, of which he kept a record for scrutiny by his line manager. He behaved as a junior should, fresh to the firm, determined to work hard to lift himself up the ladder of promotion and eventually to join the board and, all being well, to become senior enough to run the company. Then he would receive a substantial salary with travel perks and enough surplus income to buy a foreign property and own an estate in the Home Counties. That was Tom's grand plan to define his career. He would marry once he had earned enough money to buy a house and would settle down to his carefully thought-out life and to an existence of high reward for endeavour.

Bertram's ambitions were different. He was more of a countryman and would start off in the provinces, not working in an urban office but throwing himself into serving a community maybe as a social worker.

The city was not for him. He took himself north to work with the friendly but underprivileged people in the poor rural areas. He married Sally, a local girl, and bought a modest property in an attractive village. Two children later he had severed his connection with his previous life down south except for his contact with Tom. They remembered shared stories of their days at university and the laughter and parties they had enjoyed. Those memories would stay with them both. Too bad that their lives no longer converged: their friendship did, and they kept sporadically in touch, vowing to meet from time to time if ever one was in the territory of the other. Though this seldom happened, the intention was clear and any chance to meet was grabbed without hesitation. The difference in their lifestyles never became a barrier, rather the opposite in fact as each one benefited from the experiences of the other. It was a bonus that they could contribute intellectually with each other.

The only possible event which could have upset a close friendship was their meeting place. Tom was careful not to reserve a lunch table at an expensive restaurant in line with his own inclinations and level of prosperity. They would meet, when the chance to do so arose, at a pub or a modest eating house where they would both feel comfortable as they chatted about times old and new. They hardly acknowledged their different economic levels: no envy passed between them. Their relationship was too strong for that.

Meetings between the two took place at regular, though infrequent, intervals. Tom worked all hours at his city job, having to be in the office at times when the financial sector was at its most active in other parts of the world, occasionally working sleeplessly throughout the night in pursuit of making money for his international company. Only his weekends were reserved for his family: frolics outside his work commitments were seldom on offer. He was sold to the office. This sacrifice was endured for the benefit of his family's security which consisted of a constant march towards the accumulation of wealth. Nothing comes free and one of the decisions that life demands of a man is to balance the reduction of quality of life with the promise of high reward. Tom had chosen the route to the top at great personal cost with the potential reward of a prosperous middle age and a comfortable retirement. His wife Kate understood the direction he wished to go and fell in with it. His two children grew up in innocent acceptance of a father's intermittent presence. Sacrifices were hard but rewards would be great if Tom made it to the top.

The summit of Bertram's ambitions was satisfaction in his contribution to the wellbeing of mankind. From his work in social services he transferred to a teacher training course and ultimately to teaching French and German at a progressively-led comprehensive where he achieved success as a highly respected lecturer. That the teaching profession is a calling rather than a bid for financial enrichment meant that there was no big money to be made from it, but Bertram found satisfaction aplenty and he spent happy holidays with his family enjoying sports, adventure, and the pleasures of the countryside. Despite their different paths, he and Tom loyally kept in touch and each one rejoiced in the progress of the other, parted though they were by geography and opportunities to meet.

It was therefore both a surprise and a pleasure when Bertram heard that Tom was being sent north on a business trip and they would be able to meet again, maybe at one of the ordinary restaurants familiar to them from times past. There they could bring up to date discussions of their vastly different lives, work experiences and lifestyles at opposite ends of the country. This was a rare chance and each looked forward to the occasion with relish.

Tom gave instructions to his driver to arrive ten minutes before the scheduled time that he had agreed with Bertram, and to park discreetly at a distant corner of the car park. He had found it easy to exchange his tie and city suit for the more relaxed attire of tweed jacket and neutral trousers, not so much as to dress down for Bertram but rather to blend with the informal atmosphere of the Saracen's Head. It was a respectable north of England pub where he could feel at ease free from the unnatural formality he would need later that afternoon in the presence of his clients, factory owners from the prosperous industrial towns of the north.

Bertram for his part had not attempted to dress up for Tom but was content to stick to the tidy clothes he wore for teaching that would also conform to the lunchtime scene of a county inn. The two of them met in harmonious embrace delighted at seeing each other again. They ordered pints of John Smith bitter and settled down in the window of the public bar. If Bertram noticed an unusually smart limousine parked far off in the carpark, he either felt no need to remark on it or never associated it with Tom dressed as he was like an unpressurised businessman taking a good long lunch hour in the country. As the conversation flowed it was as though they had never been parted, remembering times past and, running into the present time, their families and their interests and concerns. It hardly seemed to matter that their lives had taken different routes, though it was hard to remain completely free of the differences in the earning power of each man.

Each expressed contentment with his chosen profession while modestly admitting to the extent of his workload, Bertram in marking exam papers long into the holidays, Tom for the times he worked round the clock in pursuit of financial deals. Yet, despite Tom's efforts not to show it, it could not be hidden that Tom earned an immeasurably higher salary than Bertram, who let it slip that he was saving for a new car and would have to forego the current year's family holiday. He was not moaning about it. He was accepting that his frugal life was one which he had chosen in full knowledge of the consequences and he was quite happy to congratulate Tom on his deserved success in business. Tom resisted any chance to sympathise with Bertram openly, to patronise him or to pretend that in any sense he had chosen a better route to the top, even if it could be established where 'the top' was actually to be found. He did however have a sneaking internal sympathy with his old friend and the thought that dear old Bertram and his family would be taking a much reduced holiday this year. He wished he could do something about it but felt strongly that such a thing would be impossible, for Bertram would never accept charity from an old friend and for him to provide it would only highlight his own status. It was a dilemma for Tom. He could either leave Bertram without a family holiday, or help him out at the risk of offending him. He set the idea to one side, as being beyond solution.

It was just two weeks after their happy reunion that Bertram received a letter from Tom in his own hand-writing bearing some good news. By a timely coincidence Tom's company had opened a new hotel on the south coast and were seeking guests the following month on a completely gratuitous basis as an inaugural gesture to selected guests. Tom and his wife had been chosen to spend five nights there to try it out as a 'holiday experience'. One of the other executives of Tom's firm had been unable to take up the offer and a vacancy had arisen, so Tom was writing to ask if Bertram and his wife and two children would care to join them for a short break on the south coast, entirely free of cost. Nothing would please him more, Tom wrote, than if Bertram and his family would do them the honour of trying out the country hotel. It would be doing his firm a service and into the bargain their families would have the chance to spend some real time together. Furthermore, the week in question happened to coincide with a circus and country fair which was taking place a stone's throw from the hotel, so there would be entertainment for the kids, as well as the hotel pool and the beach below. Tom had already seen the property and it was in a truly beautiful position on the cliffs overlooking the ocean. Just pray for a week of good weather and it would all be perfect.

At first Bertram was thrilled to receive such an invitation, but after a while he started to have reservations. He could not be certain if he had told Tom about the holiday he was unable to afford this year and, if he had mentioned it, whether Tom had taken it in. He could not remember Tom commenting on it or being especially responsive and so it was most likely that Tom had missed it altogether. Bertram would never consider taking charity from Tom any more than he believed Tom would wish to offer it to him. Of that Bertram was sure. He thought about it carefully. He decided to take the invitation at face value and put it down to happy coincidence. It often happens, thought Bertram, that when you have been thinking about something in your sub-conscience an event occurs unexpectedly to match your thoughts. It was like talking about a friend you haven't seen for years and then bumping into him days later—probably more than once. It's a kind of premonition… a pre-destination.

Bertram discussed the invitation with his wife. It would be the perfect break, especially for the kids, with the circus on their doorstep and all the advantages of the coast at their disposal. And from the way the invitation was worded it sounded as though they could help to promote Tom's firm by feeding back complimentary views of the hotel. In both directions the motives were clear. Tom and his wife were as keen as Bertram's family to share a few days together. Secure in his mind that this offer was nothing more or less than a business initiative from a hotel owned by Tom's firm Bertram accepted the invitation with unqualified pleasure.

Six weeks later Tom and Kate Curtis and Bertram and Sally McAdam and their respective families met in the forecourt of the hotel at the agreed time. They would get to know each other during the next five days, have meals together and relax in each other's company. It was a great idea of Tom's to recognise such a golden opportunity and decide to do something about it. Tom was obviously familiar with the hotel and was able to show his guests round the beautifully landscaped gardens. He had also arranged for Bertram's family to have two of the best interconnecting rooms, overlooking the ocean and the wide expanse of sand with no holidaymakers in sight. As they toured the grounds they noticed with interest the multi-coloured circus tents in the process of being erected in the field next door and the busy fairground attractions rising crazily into the air. It was all there for the kids, as convenient as could be. Their expectations had been fulfilled: they would make the most of a memorable week, with non-stop fun and the weather set fair.

The concierge greeted them at the front desk "Welcome to The Imperius. You have booked at just the right moment. The circus ground opens tomorrow so there will be plenty of excitements for the youngsters. It is our first season too. Not surprisingly we are fully booked for the week. Enjoy your stay with us, and let us know if we can help you in any way."

They met at the Bar that first evening high in anticipation of the days to follow. Bertram made a short speech thanking Tom for giving his family top priority to fill the holiday vacancy which had arisen in his firm. It was the gesture of a true friend, he asserted. Tom replied by assuring Bertram and his family how delighted he was that they'd had the chance of a holiday this year, even a short one. It was the first time Bertram had been sure that Tom had taken his predicament on board and he thanked him again for that, though Tom had not enlarged on the vacancy issue. The evening passed in lively conversation and an uninhibited round of drinks for the adults. The children sat at their own dining table making new friendships and chattering among themselves.

The relaxed atmosphere continued till they all retired to bed, the peace of the night enhanced by the gentle breaking of the waves on the beach below. They woke to a rising sun and cries of the seagulls setting out on the first feeding expeditions of the day. Soon human activity stirred as final preparations got under way at the fairground in the field outside their window to the clinking of hammer on metal and the diverse noises of engine-driven attractions and the faint beat of musical rides. It heralded a day of undiluted pleasure.

And such it was. Swimming in the pool was top of the list for the children. While Tom disappeared in the morning to attend to hotel business affairs, the remaining adults walked in the grounds and then fell into a swing chair on the patio to gaze out to sea and read their novels, an iced drink at their elbow. The afternoon had been reserved for the fairground. The circus date would come on the final day. All afternoon the four children played the field of events at the fair, target shooting, riding the roller coaster, crashing the dodgems, thrilling to the windmill machine which flung them around in the air. Hours of non-stop action brought them back exhausted for a meal and an early bed. It was the perfect recipe for a family break.

Just one thing had passed unnoticed which was to become evident when the parents joined them upstairs in their adjoining room. The bedroom suite of Bertram and Sally occupied one corner of the hotel with windows to the south overlooking the sea and those on the west side giving on to the fairground field. The thrills and excitements emanating from the latter which had entertained the children all afternoon were still proceeding at full power. To open the window on the west side was to fill the room with a deafening mix of throb and beat. Closing it and opening the window on the south side softened the cacophony a little but it was still too intrusive for sleep. They would simply have to wait until the licenced hours of operation ran out and fairground activities fell dead. Until then they and the children would lie awake.

As the clock signalled eleven o'clock the music stopped, and the relentless noise from the site faded away. The lights went out as though operated by a single switch and all evidence of the frantic entertainment vanished into the darkness. A sudden peace returned with the silence of the night, bringing glorious relief to the hopeful sleepers.

But the calm of the night was not to be left to the swish of the waves lapping the beach, not for long. As the fairground emptied, the sound of voices from merrymakers leaving the bar rose in an ugly crescendo as a crowd of young people moved towards the beach. For them the night was still young. The fair had provided the stimulus they needed to carry their party-going into the night. From the beach below the McAdams' window came the strains of heavy music, accompanied by shouting as voices tried to make themselves heard above the beat. Light shone out from a barbecue as the revellers settled into their spontaneous party. There was no way to stop them now. It would mean a sleepless night for the occupants of the hotel room immediately above, until dawn would come at last and the party, heedless of the disturbance they had caused, would fold and disperse, their high spirits gradually softening as they straggled their way home. For Bertram and his family it had been an uncomfortable and a distressing experience. He had considered going down to the front desk to report the matter but had decided to leave it till the morning when he could confront the manager with his sorry tale of sleeplessness.

After breakfast, taken as late as the hours would allow, Bertram stood at the front desk and asked to see the manager. To Bertram's relief, Tom had already embarked on his morning hotel duties and was happily off the scene. The wives and children had gone off to the beach, allowing Bertram a free interview with the management. The manager listened with true professional care as Bertram explained his family's experience and fear of repetition the following night. There was mutual understanding and expressions of goodwill on both sides.

"I really don't wish to complain," said Bertram. "Tom has provided this wonderful opportunity for my family to enjoy a holiday in your lovely place and the last thing I would want to do is upset him. I would be really grateful too if he never gets to hear of our conversation. I would not like him to feel we were in any way dissatisfied."

"I quite understand," said the manager, "And I wish we could change your room, but I am afraid it will not be possible. You see, we are fully booked this week. The week of the circus is about the most popular of the holiday season. Besides Mr Curtis asked specially for you to have one of our best rooms and if we were to change it he would certainly hear of it. As it is, I am obliged by my position to refer your complaint to Head Office. Every complaint has to be sent there and be dealt with by the central Complaints Department. Why, sir, if I may ask, do you not want Mr Curtis to know personally about your bad experience?"

"Well," said Bertram, feeling a bit awkward. "It's like this. Tom found a vacancy for us when someone in his firm backed out and, since they were doing a fact-finding promotion at the hotel free of charge, he kindly offered us the chance to take it up. I would not want him to think we did not appreciate his kindness."

The manager looked surprised. "You have told me something I was not aware of myself. I don't wish to contradict you, Mr McAdam, but it is not part of this hotel's policy to offer 'freebies' at this time of year, especially not at this most popular time, when the circus and fair are taking place. This is about our busiest week. According to the register all our guests are on the full tariff we apply in high season and the register tells me that all accommodation has been paid for. I could check it out but, if you do not wish me to mention this to Mr Curtis, then I shall do my best to keep it confidential. Incidentally, I have to tell you that your complaint may still come to the attention of the Board of Directors at Head Office. I shall try to direct it straight to the Complaints Department, but I cannot guarantee that it will not be leaked to the Board. I am sorry, but meanwhile I shall note what you say."

Bertram thanked the manager. He had been as open and understanding as any man could be in his position. Bertram would now report to Sally the disappointing news that nothing could be done about changing their room and, furthermore, that their experience had to be taken as a complaint and sent to headquarters, with the risk that Tom would get to hear about it. Should they own up now and risk damaging a happy atmosphere, or just cross fingers and spend the rest of their holiday with the Curtis's as if nothing had happened? It would only take a short visit into the local town to purchase some earplugs and all the following nights would become bearable. They would do everything they could to spend the remaining days with Tom, Kate and the kids in fun and harmony, culminating in a night at the circus and an evening of thanks and farewell. Apart from the unhappy start with that sleepless second night the rowdy parties outside the McAdam windows had become less intrusive, minimised by the earplugs and an acceptance of the fairground schedule.

Just one thing disturbed Bertram and Sally McAdam. It gnawed at the back of their minds and, in a quiet way, may have subconsciously inhibited their attitude or subtly changed their conduct towards their hosts. It was something that the manager had said, which had had an uncomfortable effect on them.

Could it be, just possibly, that the whole basis of the holiday—the excuse that the hotel was conducting research into its operation and was offering free accommodation to selected guests to test its performance—had been invented by Tom Curtis to give his old friend the chance of a well-deserved holiday with his family, which he would not otherwise have had? The manager certainly had had no knowledge of such a scheme. But would he necessarily have needed to know? Maybe the Board had wished the research to be kept secret from the hotel management so as not to influence its relationship with the guests.

If, the McAdams reasoned, Tom had made up the whole story, then had Tom paid for their entire holiday himself? Tom had always been a straight-forward kind of guy, totally honest. He would surely never have done such a thing without telling them and in truth he had never mentioned it. Bertram had always felt they could trust each other in every way. It was however true that Bertram himself had not entirely honoured this rule. His plea to the manager to keep his complaint hidden from Tom did not exactly conform to it, well-intentioned as it was. But then, Tom's gesture, if McAdams' theory was right, was also made with the best of intentions.

Bertram and Sally discussed the matter for some days after their return home. It concerned them that the holiday they had just taken may have been funded by Tom and, however much they argued against it, they were left with the inescapable conclusion that Tom had underwritten the entire cost of their five nights at the Imperius. There was an unhappy feeling that the relationship they had enjoyed with the Curtis's had somehow become unbalanced, that they were now in their debt and that they would never be able to repay such generosity.

This discomfiting thought nagged at them during the days that followed. What could they do for the Curtis's to relieve themselves of their perceived indebtedness? Nothing, of course, of a monetary kind. They would live with the problem without solution until the matter had passed.

True to form, it was when they least expected it that an intervening event occurred. It was in the form of a sturdy white envelope decorated with the insignia of Imperius Hotels.

The words IN CONFIDENCE were written at the top of the letter. It ran:

Dear Mr and Mrs McAdam,

You recently spent five nights at our hotel at a time when a circus and fair were taking place in the field adjoining our premises. I was very sorry to learn that your comfort and enjoyment were disturbed by excessive noise, not only from the fairground itself but also from subsequent noise arising from the unruly behaviour of individuals outside your windows. I am therefore writing on behalf of the hotel to express our sincere apologies for the inconvenience you have experienced.

As it happened, we were conducting informal research during the week in question into all aspects of our operation, it being one of the most important weeks in our calendar year, and your constructive and considered comments have been extremely helpful and of great value in shaping future policy of the hotel.

I would like to express my personal thanks to you for your contribution to our fact-finding endeavours and I hope you will pay us the honour of visiting us again at a future date when we shall have addressed the problems.

I hope you will not mind that I have headed this letter 'In Confidence'. This is because all complaints are submitted to me directly and are dealt with exclusively by this department. Names of complainants are kept strictly confidential. May I in return respectfully ask that you keep your complaint private to yourselves.

My thanks again for your help and understanding.

Yours sincerely,

Lawrence Egerton
Chief Executive, Complaints Department
Imperius Hotels

Bertram and Sally looked at each other in silence. Then relief spread across their faces. The same idea had occurred to them both. Why not invite Tom and Kate north for a reunion and take them to lunch at the Saracen's Head?

A Case of Identity

The rain drilled down on to the roofs of Sizley High Street and dripped on to the heads of the unlucky pedestrians who had failed to bring an umbrella with them. Though you could buy an umbrella cheaply at any general store along the pavement many had decided it was not worth the price and found it simpler to take refuge in a shop doorway. For Henry Ponsford the raindrops hardly seemed to matter. He was a man with a mission, a rather laboured mission since he had no exact objective in mind but he felt it necessary to keep on the move in case anything turned up. It was already past midday on Friday, clock-watchers would be getting twitchy, businesses would be preparing to close for the weekend—but still he kept hoping. In essence he was looking for a job, or some sort of occupation which would provide meaning to his existence, finding that nothing at home was of sufficient stimulation for his mind and physique. Henry had enjoyed a basic education but, there being no sixth form at the local secondary school he had attended, he had reached the end of academia. He had excelled at nothing except for a pleasing popularity among his contemporaries, appreciation from his teachers, and the development of an agreeable and polite personality which was immediately attractive to all who met him for the first time.

As Henry meandered down Sizley High Street he stopped at short intervals to look in a shop window, to check out any business premises which looked possibilities for engaging his services and to examine notices on lampposts in case anyone had posted a flyer promoting an event where he thought he could help. He had no particular preference for a job, just a few objections to occupations for which he felt entirely unsuited. He had no inclination to become a motor mechanic: no training or aptitude for welding or bricklaying, nothing within the food or hospitality sector. He knew plenty more specialisms which he would not consider and which he would certainly not be offered. But he had optimism and a micawber-ish belief that something would drop into his lap, even though he had no concept of what that might be. The rain continued to fall, steadily and gloomily, until Henry had reached the end of the street and had crossed to the other side to make his way back along the frontages of shops and offices which bore little trace of hope for the average job-seeker. But, if Henry could be described as an average youth, his attitude was far from that. It was not a matter of frantic perseverance in his case. His method was to plough on, miss no tricks, keep up his morale and wait for the pot of gold at the rainbow's end.

An actual rainbow had yet to appear on that wet afternoon and the sky had not lightened when Henry realised he had reached saturation point. His clothes had become heavy and his shoes were filling with droplets running down his trousers and seeping in through his socks. He stopped in a doorway for shelter. He had only been there a few moments when a middle-aged couple emerged from the premises, took a look at the weather and attempted to raise their umbrellas, colliding with Henry and pushing him grumpily out into the rain. There might have been room in the doorway for two people but not for three and Henry's occupancy of the porch was an obstruction to any potential clients. This was more obvious when a younger couple tried to enter the building a few moments later and were forced to lower their umbrellas in the street before brushing past Henry, rainwater dripping from their hair. It was plainly not an ideal situation for anyone and it was not surprising when the shop door opened and a young female assistant, choosing the quickest way to unblock the entrance, invited Henry in and sat him down on a plastic chair in the reception area.

For the next uncomfortable minutes Henry stared ahead, grateful for the shelter but feeling decidedly awkward, occasionally glancing up at the skylight above the door to see if the rain had stopped. The receptionist was quietly typing away stopping only to bid a smiling farewell to the couple who emerged from the office on her right. The room settled back to an embarrassed silence. Henry wondered if he should just get up and walk out but thought this would be ungracious after accepting refuge from a sympathetic young lady, reluctant though she had been to do so. Morally, he was trapped on his chair while the rain beat down outside.

The tension was eventually broken by the receptionist who, having noticed it was time for a tea-break, moved towards the kettle. Automatically treating Henry like a client waiting for his appointment she offered him a cup of tea. "Oh, thanks," said Henry, "Milk and one, please." There is nothing like a cup of tea, as experience tells us, to create a sociable atmosphere and, sure enough, it was only a matter of moments before Henry and the receptionist were exchanging relaxed conversation across the room from their separate chairs. The receptionist introduced herself as Lucy. She had been employed in her job for less than a month. Working for her boss, Hugh Bennett-Brown, had been just the opportunity she needed and she was enjoying the chance to be in at the start of a great venture as he opened a new branch of his insurance brokerage business. A substantial company this was too, her boss had told her, with branches spread around the country and its head office in Dover. This branch would undoubtedly grow as it recruited more staff and business already had taken off with countless interesting deals on offer and attractive premiums for those who could not afford the crippling cost of insuring their house and contents in a rising market. Mr Bennett-Brown had flair and enterprise. As his success had shown already, he was a man in a hurry to teach the insurance industry true business realities and how to provide a simple product without strings. Lucy had been greatly impressed by her boss's energy and compelling personality and was hoping to work her way up in the company.

As he listened to Lucy's litany of praise for her boss, Henry's mind was stirring. Recruiting more staff sounded hopeful. Could he possibly be one of the lucky ones? A job starting at the bottom was just what he was after, an opportunity he had sought for weeks. But did he stand any chance with his lack of qualifications: was this just a mirage, the fantasy of an unreal imagination? Or was it just possible that fate had put him in the right place at the right time? He wondered what Lucy felt about it. Henry had little to offer, he admitted to Lucy. He had tried for jobs without success: he had no specialist skills. All he could offer was his gratitude to anybody who could believe in him as a loyal member of a team who would work hard and turn up on time.

A door opened suddenly and from an adjoining office emerged a man in a grey suit and blue spotted tie. Smart and urbane, he appeared to be in his late thirties endowed with a sense of urgency as he dropped a document on to Lucy's desk and turned back swiftly towards his office. Lucy stopped him. "Mr Bennett-Brown, "she said, sensing that this was a time for formality, "can you spare a moment? There is a young man here who is looking for an office job [here Lucy stretched a point] and who has come in to see if you needed someone of his ability to work here." Hugh Bennett-Brown flinched slightly, then relaxed and, after a pause and a few basic questions, he motioned Henry into his office. "Bring your tea in with you," he said in a friendly mid-Atlantic accent. Henry, with an anxious mixture of hope and surprise, followed him inside. For a full half hour Lucy carried on with her work wondering at the back of her mind how this unusual and spontaneous interview would work out. She felt responsible. Was it not a bit impertinent to have forced her boss's hand into interviewing a complete stranger? If it went wrong then she would have wasted his valuable time, though as time passed she became more confident that her recommendation might have proved fruitful. If not, Henry would surely have been thrown out by now.

When he reappeared, Henry had a half-smile on his face. It was plainer still that the interview had gone well when Mr Bennett-Brown followed him briskly out of his office. "I have decided, Lucy," he said "to take this young man on for a trial period. If he turns out to be reliable after a month I shall consider him for the payroll. He can start on Monday. Please complete his formalities today and make sure he is familiar with office procedures. Henry, I'll see you Monday." With that Mr Bennett-Brown returned to his office, using an incoming call as an excuse to conclude his instructions, and closed the door.

Henry and Lucy were filling in the forms of Henry's engagement when Hugh Bennett-Brown burst out of his room. "I hadn't noticed the time," he said with an unusual sense of urgency, "I am due in London tonight for dinner at my club. I mustn't be late, or Lord Alderney will not be impressed." With that he quickly left the office leaving Lucy to spend the rest of the afternoon explaining the office rules to Henry before they left to catch their respective buses home.

Henry spent the weekend excited by his astonishingly good fortune in acquiring a real office job and the prospect of working with Lucy in the coming weeks. When Monday arrived he would make sure he was in the office on time, properly turned out in jacket and trousers, willing to throw his efforts into the work that Mr Bennett-Brown had prepared for him. Henry was already thinking about stamping his personality on the business and doing everything he could to contribute to its success. He and Lucy would make a great team: Henry was sure of that.

As Henry walked from the bus stop that Monday he looked into the windows of the neighbouring shops to acquaint himself with the street and to make a note of the business names. After walking for longer than he had expected, he stopped to take his bearings. Where was his new office? He must have passed it, how careless of him. In his desire to be on time he had gone too fast and missed it, he thought. That seemed strange because it was an imposing frontage, with enticing business offers in the window and a well-lit exterior, bold and distinctive. He turned and walked back.

He did not have far to walk before, to his relief, he noticed a familiar figure coming his way. It was Lucy, the same reassuring Lucy, but now looking decidedly shaken and flustered. Henry's relief was short-lived. "What on earth has happened?" Lucy cried out. Have you seen it—the office? It's closed. There's a notice on the door saying they have closed down the business. What the hell's going on? Do you know?" Henry stood watching her, utterly bemused. Had Lucy gone off her head? Or was she really telling him that the dream he had lived this past week had now, suddenly, vanished? He had had no experience of anything like this before. Had he entered the real world?

"It's true," Lucy gasped, as they attempted to recover their composure, "Have a look at the door. The police have been." They stood back from the shop frontage and studied it in horror. It looked quite different. Gone were the symbols of confidence, the welcoming notices, the lighted windows, the trappings of honesty and security that had so recently enticed hopeful investors inside the premises. Instead, the windows were bare and unlit. There was no indication that this was a place of business, just a notice on the door in bold black print: **CLOSED All enquiries to Detective Inspector Rushmore, Fraud Squad, Sizley Police Station**. A request for information from the public was written underneath.

Lucy and Henry looked at each other in silence, then together they walked slowly along the street before drifting into a coffee shop to review the situation that had so suddenly shattered their lives. In disbelief they sat drinking coffee, wondering what the future now held for them. For long minutes they remained in shock till reality gradually started to take over. "We must face up to this," said Lucy, "our next move must be to see the police and find out what is happening. I doubt we can tell them much, as they will know a lot more than we do. I can't believe that Hugh Bennett-Brown has been caught up in some scam. It must be terrible for him. I'd call him if I knew his number but I never really knew where he lived either. He often mentioned his family but they never came to the office which, I suppose, is not surprising since he was always so busy."

By appointment, Lucy and Henry arrived at Sizley Police Station the following day and were shown into the office of Peter Rushmore, Detective Inspector and fraud investigator. They studied each other over a bare wooden desk in an atmosphere formal but unthreatening. "I understand," said the detective, "that you were both employed by the man we know as Hugh Bennett-Brown, is that correct?" Henry explained nervously that he had not yet started work at the office. "I see", said Mr Rushmore, "then you didn't know that your prospective employer was being investigated for fraud on a very serious scale and that the police were trying to establish his identity? Unfortunately he must have got wind of our movements and disappeared before we could close in on him. Bennett-Brown was certainly not his real name. He trades under a number of aliases, so maybe even he no longer knows who he is. We have no home address for him and believe he used a string of local hotels, signing the register in different names. There is a substantial reward on offer for information leading to his arrest. Perhaps you can tell me anything you know about his private life or the places he visited. Have you any information which might help us?"

Henry looked blank. He had a good memory for names and faces but none of that would be relevant as he possessed no photograph of Mr Bennett-Brown—and that wasn't his name in any case. "I may be able to help," Lucy remembered. "When he left the office in a hurry last Friday he mentioned he had a date at his club in London and could not be late." "What is the name of his club?" asked the detective. "He had never mentioned the club before so I don't know the name of it," Lucy replied, "though he said he was having dinner that night with Lord Alderney, I'm sure that was the name. He must be able to help. He would have seen him later than any of us." Mr Rushmore opened a drawer in his desk and took out a thick black book which he riffled through, before studying a page in detail. Then he closed the book and replaced it in the drawer. "That is helpful," he said, "but he is unlikely to assist our investigation, I'm afraid. Lord Alderney does not exist."

As the weeks passed without any break-through in the investigation, the dejection Lucy felt at having seen her loyalty betrayed by a man in whom she had placed her trust started to melt away. That she had fallen for a chronicle of lies from an unashamed crook did not seem to count against her any longer. She was the one who had remained faithful while her former boss had fed her with absurd stories about his successful business ventures, torn from the depths of his imagination. She might have even felt sorry for him had she not been mindful of the grief and chaos he had brought to the lives of others and, in a different way, to the hopes of Henry Ponsford whose first job had ended before it had begun. In short, Lucy was recovering from her disappointment and had hit upon the idea of letting out the spare room in her flat to tourists on a weekly basis to provide a modest income. She wondered how Henry was getting on.

Lucy was never far from Henry's thoughts, either. He wondered what she was doing. He had not felt easy about contacting her since the day his means of subsistence had been torn from him. He had taken a job in an estate agency, but only on a commission basis, which produced hardly enough to feed himself. He hated the job in any case but could not escape from the office to search for another. There was little he could offer Lucy in the shape of security. All he could do was persevere as he had always done, keep his eyes open and his hopes high. So when he received a call from Lucy his spirits soared. They would meet again—in the coffee shop to which they had adjourned on that fatal day.

Over coffee they talked little about the collapse of the business they had once trusted. That was now history. They said nothing about Mr Bennett-Brown and his fraudulent dealings. They did not dwell on the past but discussed the present and their hopes for the future. The longer their meeting lasted the stronger grew the bond which fate had reserved for them. That a disaster often creates an opportunity for a change of direction is well-established philosophy. They both recognised that. A few days spent together in the countryside or wandering along an empty beach would be what was needed to test this theory. Lucy offered to find a quiet boarding house in a seaside resort on the west coast where they could relax, clear their minds and enjoy a new dream removed from the confusion of everyday life.

Stratton Sands is a respectable resort with the standard terrace of Edwardian guesthouses overlooking the promenade, with benches well-spaced for gazing out to sea. The expanse of beach is clean and clear and one of the most picturesque in that part of the country. It has traditionally been a haven for those who have no need for pleasure gardens or bright lights. What keeps the resort free from crowds is its lack of a mainline station with only a single-track branch line to serve the liberal collection of intimate privately owned hotels in the area. It is a town where couples of all ages go to switch off and enjoy a stretch of natural coastline. As a place for romance it is ideal.

And that was what Lucy and Henry found during their short break in the Rockpool Guesthouse on the front. They had quickly become familiar with the layout of the town, the quaint shops and the network of walks to remote corners of the beach. They had reached their third day and it was almost time to return home. It was late on their final morning when they left their lodgings to explore the remaining part of the town that they had not yet visited, which took them on a route past the station. One of the few trains of the day had just pulled in and a trickle of new arrivals was emerging from the entrance hall. It was a routine event to any passer-by, except that the sight of one member of the small group caused Henry to stop dead. He was certain he knew the face... not quite the same face he had once seen at close quarters across a desk: it was now wearing a moustache, but its physical features were the same. He motioned Lucy to stare at the figure. Yes, it was him... surely it was... unmistakably him, the man who, accompanied by a young woman, now dived into the first taxi on the rank and was driven away.

Forget the shock, this was a time for cool heads. Henry and Lucy sat on the grass and worked it out. Where had the man gone? Raking back in their heads what the Detective Inspector had told them, they remembered that he had a liking for hotels. He never used his real name, whatever that was, so he certainly would not be checking in as Hugh Bennett-Brown, if indeed he was checking into a hotel at all. Maybe he had his own home down here, though from the way he moved around, he had behaved like a man of no fixed address. They could telephone all the hotels in the area one by one to ask if he was staying there but, since they did not know his name, that would be pointless. There was only one chance, a very faint one, but a chance nonetheless.

Later that day Henry, armed with a comprehensive list of the local hotels, started out on his exercise of discovery. He drew a blank with the first five hotels he called. When he called the sixth, a gentleman at reception answered, "The Linley Hotel". "Good evening," said Henry, "do you by any chance have a Lord Alderney staying with you?" "I don't believe so", said the man on the desk. "I'll just check the register. Who shall I say is calling?" "My name is Henry Ponsford," said Henry unguardedly. There was a pause, then sudden enthusiasm, "Oh, good evening, Mr Ponsford, I'm so sorry, I didn't recognise your voice at first" said the man on the desk, "It's very good to hear from you again, sir. I gather you will be staying with us later in the week. Bear with me a moment and I'll see if Lord Alderney is staying with us tonight." "No, don't bother now," said Henry, in his best mid-Atlantic accent. He rang off.

He and Lucy smiled at each other. "When we ring Mr Rushmore," said Henry, "we might ask if that reward is still on offer". Lucy nodded.

THE END